FUTURE PASTIMES
IN A NEW
WORLD ORDER

FUTURE PASTIMES IN A NEW WORLD ORDER

A Science Fiction Novel

by

RAY WILLS

(The Gypsy Poet)

ISBN: 9798423077037

POETIC LICENCE

I got my poetic licence
it came to me in a flash
in subtle understanding
in prose and words so fast

I jotted down the meanings
the lines they were unique
in common understanding
my intellect took a leap

I got my lines of eloquence
the poets friend in trust
the metaphors were grounded
in reverence and praise
the lines flowed
in rhythmic interludes
i had to be so brave

The flow it was tremendous
written down in verse
the words were common intellect
its voice so unrehearsed

I wrote of love and symmetry
the mistress of my past
my future it was grounded
my licence its so splendid
I knew it was to last

At least that's what im told
though the words just came on fashion
imagery and prose

Ray Wills

CONTENTS

ABOUT THE AUTHOR

Ray Wills was born in Newtown Poole Dorset in 1945. Rays childhood and early youth was spent in Dorset on the Mannings Heathland in Poole. Where he lived next door to the Dorset councils Gypsy traveller encampment. Then later in his childhood he moved home to live at Wareham in Dorset.

After leaving school at Kemp Welch school in Poole. His first job was as a painter decorator and chassis sprayer for Bluebird Caravans. The largest caravan industry in the world. Than he moved to live at Bovington Army camp in Wareham Dorset. Where he was employed as an Officers Batman. Before joining Community Service Volunteers in the mid 60s.Which was the British branch of Voluntary Service Overseas. One of Rays first placement at C.S.V was for Redditch District Council as holiday play schemes leader. Due to his success there the council seconded him for training in Play leadership at Play Field House home of the National Playing Fields Association where he was based at Notting Hill Adventure Playground, Holland park play park and Battersea in London.

He continued to work closely with the National Playing Fields Association for many decades working for numerous local councils and voluntary play associations in the UK. Establishing and managing countless children's adventure playgrounds and play projects in many of the inner cities and rural communities throughout the UK over 4 decades. In recent years as a social activist he led many campaigns and chaired numerous community and tenant groups nationally . Working closely with local councils including Bournemouth where he was at one time a parent school governor and laired closely with the Housing Department. Prior to working with adults with severe learning disabilities as a support worker in Dorset.

Ray Wills is a poet,writer and social historian. He has been a member of numerous poetry groups as well as being an authority on the history of the Gypsy community. He is at present project leader at Kushti Bok the Gypsy Roma Traveller welfare organisation.

His qualifications include a Royal Society of Arts Diploma in Management at Degree level and a Senior Youth worker City and Guilds Award certificate. At present he lives within a community of artists, writers and musicians in the village of Bere Regis in Dorset. Here he continues to give talks on local history and poetry readings throughout Dorset. He works closely with Poole and Dorchester Museums, Bournemouth Central and West Howe libraries and the Dorchester Heritage centre and Shire Hall. Where he has been involved in Exhibits on behalf of Kushti Bok the Gypsy Roma Traveller welfare organisation. He also is admin of numerous community organisation pages on Facebook on child's play international and Gypsy Travellers in Dorset. He regularly contributes articles for both the Traveller Times and Play and Playground magazines.

ACKNOWLEDGEMENTS

The author is indebted to the following:

Susan Miller and Brian Cordell for their support and encouragement throughout.

PREVIOUS PUBLICATIONS

Ray Wills previous publications have included the following.

THE LAST STOPPING PLACE- Available at AMAZON

THE TIME TRAVELLER - Available at AMAZON

GYPSY TALES - Available at AMAZON

THE GYPSY CAMP - Available at AMAZON

ADVENTURES IN CHILDS PLAY - Available at AMAZON

THE CANFORD CHRONICLES a poetry Anthology- Available at LULU

ROMANCE IN THE EVERGLADES poetry Anthology- published by xpress publications.

WHERE THE RIVER BENDS - Available at LULU

THE GYPSY STORYTELLER Anthology was published by Francis Boutle Publisher, At present out of print.

CONTACTS FOR ADVICE AND INFORMATION
IN THE COMMUNITY Handbook.
Which was a NATIONAL PLAYING FIELDS Publication.

DORSET DAYS Poetry Anthology Available from Amazon

FUN DAYS IN POOLE Poetry Anthology Available from Amazon

Ray Wills has also contributed numerous articles for many books and periodicals.

Including the following
On Birmingham's adventure playground Balsall Heath For General Public org UK.
Entitled LET US PLAY.
Regular Articles for the Gypsy Traveller magazine Traveller Times.

He manages many Facebook pages
These include
DORSET GYPSY TRAVELLERS.

MEMORIES OF THE PURBECK.
And
THE INTERNATIONAL HISTORY OF CHILDS PLAY.

INTRODUCTION

THE NEW WORLD EXPRESS

All aboard the new world express
take your seat next to mine but don't cough or jest
there's a new life tomorrow wear your mask with pride
stand in the queue to the greatest divide

All aboard the political chain
take along your Grandma
take the new test
treat life with caution be alert be curt
follow your leaders
take the words they say
science is king just for today

All aboard the new world express
keep your truth close to your chest
you know its best
all aboard the country ride
beachcombers undignified

Prepare for the independence day
stand in line the cures at hand
these are crowded times
stand in line
all aboard the new world express.

Ray Wills

NEW WORLD

What sort of world are they creating
what kind of dreams do they inspire
what sort of heartaches are they shaping
guess theyl be around awhile

What kind of thoughts were they thinking
in the shadows of their minds
what kind of world are they creating
I guess we l know in time

What sort of world will they surrender
to the pockets of the few in time
so many hungry children
so many dreams to not come true
what kind of songs will they be singing
in the future yet to be for me and you

What kind of world are they creating
why don't you know and not ask me
what sort of world are they creating
with their misfits and all their lies
all their political persuasions
from ten to thirty nine

What kind of leaders are we following
will they lead us all astray
with their thoughts and aspirations
will we all wake up someday

Ray Wills

I wrote this story following the corona virus pandemic which swept the world in 2019. This was my response to the horror which took so many lives not only in the UK but throughout the world. I have put together a what if science fiction story in the mould of Aldous Huxley and George Orwell. Its a novel that looks at our present position and our heritage. It explores the world we created through the Industrial revolution and the concerns about Global warming and the results of the measures we took in 2021. It looks at the issues of risks in our society along with the loss of childhood and the changing face of the sexual revolution. Feminism, gay rights and gender bending. As well as health and safety measures and many other issues. Its a world created through the development of the New World Order and it questions our intent and our future.

Our story is set in the far distant future. A young Gypsy Terry Hughes is involved in a New World Order organisation. He is a firm believer of its philosophy and follows all of its ways religiously. Then he stumbles over Ben Boswell in a prohibited zone and it was there he falls madly in love with Ben's daughter Ruby. Then through her he discovers an underground secretive and prohibited society. A society where workers are still involved in old industries such as brickworks, potteries and the use of coal. Which are all practices prohibited by the organisations modern society. Then he meets a young girl Mary Donnelly and through her he uncovers a children's playground world. Where endless risks are undertaken and yet all of its child members are profoundly happy despite their social circumstances. Then after he had officially followed his musician friend in the organisation for a number of years. he uncovers real truths behind the organisation itself. Truths which changes his views of his world and sets him free and on a course of self discovery and change. After coming to the realisation that things within the organisation itself are not as they all seem. After many setbacks and shocking discoveries he works on a ingenious plan to change things for the benefit for all of the people. The book is complimented with an assortment of my poetry throughout.

CHAPTER ONE

BIRD SONG

BIRD SONG

He had him a life in the tree tops
he had him a voice that could sing
he had him a vision
and he flew on the wing

He had him a crows nest
he had him a mate
he had him some young birds
some chicks
and he sang on your gate
like some olé guitar licks

He had him some journeys
he had him some flights
he had him a travelling
by day and by night

He had him a story
he had him a tale
he had him a romance
a darling as well

He had him some travelling
he took him some flights
he sang him some songs there
to make the world feel so right

Ray Wills

LAB DREAMS

I studied science, psychic and the soil
got my hands burnt in the vacuum
in another world
I travelled in the circuit
which transverses all my dreams
but life was just illusion
full of hopes and screams

The epicentre welcomed me
in the canyon of the mind
the crowds they cheered and gathered
though some were not the loving kind

The social distance followers
they all went there all in line
some wore masks and spoke in dreams
others walked the line

The labs were opened wide that day
the bats had flown always
the rumours were demented
but wouldn't go away

I stumbled into consequence
he was banging on his drum
reading all the headlines
writ out for the dumb

Was it all a consequence
of some man's wanton dreams
created in a test tube
planted in life's stream

I spoke out to the universe
but they stole it from the web
Big Brother was in charge that day
all life was rearranged he said

Ray Wills

FREEDOM CHANTS

When morning broke in the land of the free
when the hands of the clock moved
it was the time for liberty
the anarchic fools studied the law
then resolved their complex science
in a rhyme with no words

Where once the padre quoted the bibles prayers
whilst foolish virgins climbed the stairs
whilst the jackals barked at the break of the day
whilst all Gods children looked for a place to play

The lost soldiers wandered o'er barren lands
where oil rich sultans set their plans
though the square and compass they set the rules
for wayward boys and girls and forgetful fools
The band played its final march
as politician's played their games in the dark
the wars were over they said 'was true
as they stored more weapons
in the hands and minds of fools
The quarrelsome doctors branded anew
their potent drugs to solve the blues
whilst a lonesome crooner sang his song
the pretty dancing girls paraded with nothing on

The curtain fell and the act was through
as mankind threw out the golden rule
along with babies yet to die
whilst the clown he smiled and winked an eye

All across the world of spin
the actors bowed and the set begins
the speech that the prophet read out loud
for greedy men lost in sin

Ray Wills

A s he walked through the heart of the city Terry Hewes admired
the architecture and the technology of this new age. The noisy
polluted world of his forefathers was long gone and the traffic
much of it above ground level although very busy was noiseless.
All this had happened in his lifetime. He could never recall the
world of his father and grandfather. He was told on the screens
which were installed in all of the buildings and living quarters. The
screens told him that the world had changed considerably and he
thought all for the better. The great man made plagues of the past
had all been eliminated. Mainly by the yearly mandatory
inoculation's given out by the world government from childbirth. A
virus with its many mutations which over a number of years had
killed millions worldwide and 5 million in this country alone. We
had a secure society now he thought, no longer were there wars and
acts of terrorism which had plagued the world for past generations.
No longer were there such ideologies as communism, or fascism,
in fact no isms. All religions too which were built on fear and
indoctrinations all these were eliminated forever. He believed that
the world was a much better place now. Looking on the screens he
had discovered about the pagan rituals of the past and the
Catholicism. He was thankful that we were secure and cared for
now as never before as we now lived in a free society. Our New
World Order protected all individual throughout their lifetime. Men
and women were the same although physically different. It was
now a gender less society. Education was by means of the screens
for the old systems were proved to be inadequate and costly.
Employment in drudge occupations of great stress and physical
demands on bodies were long since eradicated. We were fortunate
to have all the physical work undertaken in factorial establishments
by android robot's. All of which were controlled by the main central
computer regime of Happy Euphoria. He felt privileged to be a
member of this community support organisation. An organisation
which was established to encourage and facilitate individuals into
the larger state brotherhood aptly called Happy Euphoria.

Each morning he checked into on the screen in his modern
apartment. With all facilitates on his computerised operated
programme. All were part of the nations clean energy grid. His
employment was co ordinates by the system and his role within the

organisation to encourage and facilitate its members. He felt fortunate to live in a society where green growth was encouraged, with much of the city and the country was now forestry. This had been encouraged with the growth of the need for card paper packaging and away from the earlier times of the plastics society's. Such plastics which were poisoning the natural environment. The organisation now was able to change weather patterns and to destroy toxins. Toxins which killed both man and nature. All meals were all regulated, for perfect nutrition was paramount. All was based on scientific knowledge of nutrition and the energies of our bodies. Terry just like everyone else received cooked meals from the meals computer at set tines throughout the day. No longer was high cholesterol a problem now that such diets were introduced and mandatory. No longer were there such things as diabetes or heart disease. We were a healthy society. Each part of the city was a zone. Each with its own name and number of reference.

Today Terry Hewes was making his way walking across to the south of the city to visit his close friend and mentor Brian Deleaux. Brian lived in the area which was now known as the bird zone. An area which Terry was told had once in centuries past been within the historical docklands of the city known as Canary Wharf. An area where only the rich business community lived. Now however it was an area where only the wealthiest of musicians lived. Here these maestros made music on their digital platforms. From symphonies and classical concertos to the wild rock sounds of the 20th and 21st^t centuries, afore the great plague hit the nation and the world. Music was now given its rightful place in society, as a source of well being to ones health. It was recognised as true education. Just as much as the Gymnasiums in the past were necessary and fitted out with only the best of equipment. Even as a young man now, in the prime of his life, he felt grateful to the system. As a child his parents had taught him self respect and to always follow the guidance of the Happy Euphoria order. He had been told that in the earlier days and prior to the great plague. People were living under many tyrannical governments. There were certain rights or rules which individuals had to ensure they kept to. It was a far different world then, even a time when things were crazy and well before the modern thinkers of Happy Euphoria.

When those crazy social reformers and false leaders of that past age had filled their minds with new extremist religions. He had heard via the screen that there were those who encouraged such terrible things, Things which were known as gender bending and the rights of all people to protest and carry arms. He had heard of the great conspiracies which existed then. In a time when the internets social media networks ruled many aspects of peoples lives and thinking. During those times young not yet mature adults had been permitted and encouraged to spend free time in idle pursuits. Such pursuits were then referred to as child's play. For centuries it had been this way, until just prior and before the plague took its toll. Then initially in those days the new rules of health and safety came into force and fortunately much of these dangerous risky idle pursuits were gradually banned. Then the plague with its restrictions, lock downs and safety laws was to thankfully eradicate these time wasting and risky activities completely from the minds and bodies of young people. He had been told and educated on the screens also that people were previously in those earlier times, set back in their development. They were categorised by gender. However nowadays fortunately we had all of the people involved together as equals, alongside one another. Now each person was an individual, both male and female in all activities and interactions. No longer were there male or female only sports teams and activities. Whether soccer, rugby, cricket,or dancing sessions. No longer were there separate public conveniences so cutting costs and unnecessary waste. For now both genders male and female took part in all of these as team members together side by side. He thought it so wrong that they were in past times denied the obvious, for to him it was unbelievable. As he walked through the streets of his home zone he recognised the landmarks of this modern age. All of the prominent statues of the city,along with the large community screens. Screens which continually showed the great advances which had evolved over recent decades. The weather today was sunny, warm and with a clear light blue sky. This was another area in life which the new order had improved life for its people with weather changing scientific improvements. It was now afternoon, his wrist watch timer bleeped 1300 hours. He was aware that he was being watched as all were. It was so good that people were

7

watched over and protected by the organisation. With one of the street screens displaying the area were he was now presently walking. It proudly showed all of the modern buildings,architecture and the statues of its modern leaders. Terry Hewes friend Brian Deleaux was expecting him. The Mansions where Brian lived was within what was known as the bird zone and it was exquisite. All the apartment buildings here were made from white marble with its high walls surroundings. Here there were strong metal iron gates protecting the buildings itself along with their well hidden CCTV cameras. As he approached his friends apartment he knew that Brian would be pleased to see him. Although Brian was a more mature man being in retirement, but still involved with creating his music as a hobby. He had known Brian since first he had been initiated into the organisation as a pioneer sub member of Happy Euphoria just a few years ago. As he approached Brian's apartment he saw that it was surrounded by a variety of trees. Their many green leaves here all were full of the chatter and song of young songbirds,mainly gold finches. Such birds were a delight in both plumage as well as unique song. He walked up the ramp to the heavy metal gate outside of Brian's apartment and pressed the bell. The noise from the gold finches now was deafening, but very musically beautiful. Then the gate to Brian's apartment swung open allowing him to make his way into Brian's driveway. As he reached Brian's main door. Over it he saw its familiar bird crest emblem of an Eagle in flight with two sparrows on it wings. The emblem of the organisation. Then he heard Brian's familiar voice "Come in Terry". Then the door too swung open.

Brian greeted him with a warm hand shake and the familiar organisations salutation of a cross arm gesture. Brian said,"Come through Terry". "Did you have any difficulty finding the place?" he asked. Terry smiled and answered him, "no Brian, your directions were perfect". Brian beckoned him into his apartment, "Come and take a seat Terry, make yourself at home". "Its so good to see you outside of the screen" he said. They both smiled then Terry replied "Yes I must say Brian I was looking forward to seeing you again too,its been a while". Then Terry asked him "Hows it been since your retirement Brian?". Brian answered"Well to tell you the truth Terry I think im more busy now than when I was working n the employ for the organisation". Then Brian said"Sorry,how impolite of me would you like a drink Terry?". Terry replied "yes please Brian, have you got any lemon?" he asked. Brian answered him, "yes of course, il just pop next door." When Brian had left the room Terry looked around and saw that it was like most apartments in this age. Being very small with just a few box chairs, both comfortable with light leather with oak style edges. There was the familiar screen built into the wall which was the normal for all apartments. The screen was on an off mode at the present time. Just then Brian returned with a glass of lemon and handed it to him. Terry smiled and took it from him." Thanks Brian". "I have really come to hear some of your music and see what your up to?" he said. Brian sat down and answered him. "Well my friend, as you know, I write or compose my own stuff on there." He pointed to the screen. He then went on a long discourse of where in his opinion music had evolved. He looked intently at Terry as he spoke and said "Terry, you know of course that the old times musical classics were a mixture of orchestral music, folk and contemporary, all developed over many centuries". "Those musicians played on numerous instruments, initially to entertain the wealthy or statesmen." "Whilst others of them were church organ players, or simple musicians who played in church's for the religious groups.". " As you will see Terry, I have categorised my own library of all these great traditions here". "Even those prior to our present sound systems of our organisations". "I have categorised all of the classics, the symphonies, concertos, overtures, waltzes, operas, etc." "Including the greats such as Mozart, Beethoven, Bach, Strauss, Listz, Brahms and Vagner". "I have then studied the more simplistic, uncomplicated musical lyrical composers such as Zimmerman ,Lennon McCartney Rodgers and Hammer-stein,I found a great many of these had similarities and I have been able to trace the main rhythms, structures and create fresh musical symphonies." He continued his talking. "These which i have managed to put together, the best of these into melodies which all can enjoy". "In fact Terry im actually proud that I have found the root of such initiation is via ones creative imagination". "You should know what I am referring to Terry, with your own ancestral roots". "For didn't you discover from your own DNA that you come from Gypsy Roma?". Terry answered him "Yes your right and correct Brian", "I did discover my great ancestors were once road travellers and played many instruments, often playing music to enrich their soul". Brian laughed "Ha ha",then he said "So there you go my friend you understand the importance of my work then". Terry nodded at his friend. Then he watched as Brian then got up from his seat and went over to his screen and directly spoke into it. He said,"Start Robert" and then directly on his instruction the screen lit up automatically. Then a cultured voice from within it asked "What service do you require master.?" Brian answered "Equaliser, music Robert". At once a coloured moving equaliser graph appeared on the screen and music from within the screen played a fanfare of melodies.

By the time Terry had left Brian's apartment Brian had given him some understanding and grounding of music matter. He also had in the course of their discussions advised him not to talk outside the organisation about Brian's important work within the organisation. As he had left Brian apartment, Brian had also warned him that there were parts of the city which were prohibited and therefore out of bounds to everyone including organisation members.

CHAPTER TWO

THE COLD BLOW LANE

DICKENS DAY

The streets of Southwark were dark and grey
in the hovel homes where children played
the workhouse stood on mint street lanes
close by the old curiosity shop
where Pickwick papers here were sold again

The dockside cranes the barges boats
the rats and fame
the ships came in to the Thames
and then we walked the streets
down to cold blow lane

The cobbled streets with horse and carts
the landed gentry from Knightsbridge wealth
the Smithy shod the horses then
where cockney lads all nicked
the neckerchiefs of gents
and old watch chains

Amidst the poor and desolate folk and crime
the foggy mist the dirt and grime
the TB cough and gamblers gains
the barrel boys of market fame
as told in Oliver's life
in the theatre Drury lane
but the Greenwich park
was Lewisham gain

Dickens fame was yet to be
with great Expectations
'neath splendid trees
of oaken branches in splendid leas
he had it all with cups of tea
then we read his books of tragedies

Ray Wills

TRESSPASSERS WILL BE PROSECUTED

Please be aware
trespassers will be prosecuted
the notice read
you go here at your own risk
you cannot be led

The wording was so prominent
yet the message was in script
written in the parchment lines
and its faded black and transcript lisps

The warning held no strange affairs
for lovers yet to be
its solemn words were less inclined
to save humanity

He loved her that was obvious
but he didn't heed the pleas
he trusted in his intellect
like a ship all lost at sea

He scrambled to her side that night
though the stars were drawing fast
the moonlight set his course
his thoughts were swift and fast

He held her and he kissed her
but before he ever knew
his world was upside down that night
like Napoleon met his Waterloo

The candle burned in darkness
then he stumbled through the mire
he found her reckless as a child
though her love was sweet and wild

He often wished he'd met her back then
so long in the past
but the words of love were sweeter now
and the music a sweeter craft

Like lovers now and long ago
he held her in his arms
the clock struck twelve and recklessly
he discovered all her charms

The time went back so swiftly then
and the shooting star went by
but they were lost in wonder then
in a never ending song comply

Her kisses were deep and magical
and their passions rose to sprite
as he loved her on her feathered bed
till the dawning shed its light

He was now king of heaven
set upon his throne
the words were cast in rhetoric
and the notice now expired in tone

They walked together hand in hand
their truths were free and wild
the warnings were torn asunder then
and the shadows cast their spell so wide

Like the morning mists
they shared that day
they blossomed and were set free
free from the warnings of the past
their lives were built on liberty

Ray Wills

After leaving Brian's apartment Terry Hewes made his way out of the Mansions. As he did so he thought over the many things which his friend had said. Terry had never fully appreciated music as an education until now. It had never been his thing, or as his vocation as a young man. From the time he left school and joined the organisation own young pioneers Happy Euphoria he had immersed himself into mathematics and calculations. This was expected of him. For it was where his father had previously held a prominent position for many years. Terry respected Brian and his friendship was important to him. During their recent time together Brian had attempted to teach Terry the basics of music. Terry found the subject fascinating now, particularly the depth of the subject and the way Brian enthused it. As Terry left the mansions Brian had also given him distinct directions back to the city centre. Advising him again and again to be extra careful. For whatever he did it was imperative that he did not enter into any prohibited zone on his way home.

As he walked home Terry was deep in thought as he strolled down the side streets and back towards the direction he had originally came from. He was thinking through his time with Brian. He was going through the musical keys, the rising and falling of the chords on the equaliser screen and he was whistling the various tunes he could recall as he did so. He was so engrossed in his actions that he didn't notice the man who was laid out on the kerbside and he thus stumbled over him and almost fell over his body. As he stumbled over the man the man spoke."Watch were your going mate, this here is my territory" he said. "you look where your going mush". The man looked up at Terry and then swore at Terry. These were swear words which Terry knew of but he'd never heard uttered in his home or within or amongst his many groups of friends. The man swore again, "Fuc off you didykye, your not welcome in these parts". Terry now saw that the man laying there was around middle age. He was bearded and his clothes were of wool and a mixture of cheap cotton. His cheap looking boots had no laces only course string and he smelt of a strange foul aroma.

Terry spoke " Sorry sir" he said. Then he asked the man "Did I hurt you sir?". The man answered him, "no ya didn't mush, have you a light"? he asked. Terry replied "You don't need a light sir, for its broad daylight here and still not dusk yet". Then Terry looked down at his wristwatch and saw it read 1700 hours. The man stared at him strangely now and then he spoke again. "I meant a light for me fag, you idiots" he said. It was then that Terry saw that the man held a small piece of rolled paper in his right hand sticking out between two of his fingers. Terry asked him, "What is that in your hand sir?" he asked. The man grunted something unintelligible, then said "its a fag, you dinnlow, you not seen a fag afore?". Then he said "Its gone out. cant you see, i need a light". Terry looked at the small roll of paper in the man's hand again, then it dawned on him where he'd seen this before. He recognised it as a cigarette from a film on his screen and replied"No ive not, but i know that they are cigarettes and are banned due to their great addiction for they have killed millions in the olden times". "I don't carry matches either"he sad. The man laughed at this remark of Terry's and he said "Blimey where the ell you been mister, your not from round these ere parts be you?". "No im not" Terry replied. With this, the man stood up or at least he tried to, as he somehow gathered himself together and stood. With his shabby clothes protruding from his fat stomach and his hair ruffled beneath a brown woollen hat Terry thought he looked a right sight. Then Terry saw the bottle sticking out of the man's coat pocket and saw that its label read best stout pale ale. He knew from watching the education films as a child on the great education centres screen that these ales were very bad for ones health. For they contained high levels of toxins, alcohol poison and they caused all manner of illnesses and craziness amongst the old nations of the world. Terry knew that these ales were also prohibited under the New World Order. Terry looked closely at the man who was now stumbling around as if his legs couldn't support him. He asked the man "what's your name sir?". The man replied " its none your business, watts it to you any ways,? you wanna fight"? he said. With that he raised both hands, clenched them both each one into fists and pointed them towards Terry's face. It was then that the man lost his balance completely,he stumbled and completely fell over his own feet onto the kerb. Then he swore again "bugger me" he said. Terry asked him, "Where do you live man?", "its none your business", he replied. Terry spoke." Well you need help, come on man il help you" and Terry lifted him up to his feet."Lean on me" he said.

So it was that the stranger somewhat reluctantly leant on Terry and directed Terry towards his home. They were now in an area totally unknown to Terry with its dark old alleyways and side walks. The air here smelt thick with ash. After walking for about ten minutes he asked the man. Terry spoke "Are we near your place yet mister ?" he asked. The man looked around. then with a puzzled expression followed by a look of pleasure he said "its down that ere lane look" and he pointed to the far right. Terry helped him to walk and then arm in arm they made their way further down the rough cobbled lane where the man had earlier indicated. They were now under a low red bricked bridge. Then Terry saw the small white metal roadside notice alongside the low brick wall nearby. The sign read "COLD BLOW LANE". Terry recognised the name for it was where the one time football team of the past, known as Millwall was said to have played in the Den. He remembered it had a terrible reputation there for street fighting and hooliganism. All part of the old decades centuries ago. The lane was dark and foreboding and the cobbled stones of the narrow road were hard on ones feet. Terry knew it was in an area once known as Deptford and Millwall. However what he didn't see, being too busy guiding the drunk, was the larger modern very official sign overhead which read, "PROHIBITED" with the words below it which stated "This area is out of bounds. Any person entering here from any zone, does so at their own risk". But Terry was too concerned for the man's well being to notice the sign. They hurried together along the lane. With the man directing Terry towards a row of red brick buildings. Bricks and buildings such like Terry had never seen in recent times. Each of these brick dwellings sported a china pot on their tiled roofs,from which dark smoke was bellowing out high into the night sky. Terry knew that such a spill of smoke was illegal in these modern times. The air here was full of the smell of ash. Terry had seen pictures of such places in the screens educational programmes in his pioneer days. He knew that such places had heating from open fires in which illegal coal was burnt. This practice had been outlawed in the 21st century by the vast majority of nations and electricity generation and other alternatives were implemented under a New world Government agreement. The man caught Terry's look and responded and said. "That be our fire, me misses will be missing me". "I Got her a bottle of the best stuff here in me pocket". He gestured to the bottle sticking out from his jacket pocket. He said "We can share this tonight with some cheese and crusty rolls at our table". He led Terry in through the front door of his home and called out "you here me luv?". Just then a short stout middle aged woman of attractive homely appearance stood in front of them. "Where the ell you been Ben?" she asked. " I had your dinner on and had to throw it a ways when ya never came home" she said. Then she saw Terry and said "and whose this young Gypsy?". Terry was surprised by her last remark for he had never before been referred to as a Gypsy. The man Ben Boswell answered his wife. "I been alright woman, just me rheumatism played up and I fell over". "I fell in the gutter in the city zone and I was lucky I wernt picked up by the zone official's". "Fortunately this ere gent happened to be there and brought me home me luv."His wife responded, "Don't you luv me Ben Boswell" she said " I wont ave any your malarkey Ben", she said "I wont have it you hear" "you had too much to drink again". Then she spoke to her husband again but this time in a more friendly softer tone, "cmon Ben get that coat off and sit down, whilst il put the kettle on and we l have a nice cuppa tea,cause I expect this young Gypsy gent will appreciate a cuppa". Terry responded, "why yes thank you" he said. The woman then spoke to him directly "Sit down then my son and il rustle up some nice cheese rolls to have with your tea". Terry did as he was told and he made his way to the large table. As he did so he looked around the room and he noticed the room was a lot bigger here than any apartment room he'd ever known and which he was used to. Then he saw the fire with its logs burning and the flames and lumps of red hot coals and it made him feel so good inside. He'd never felt or had such pleasure. For the room felt warm and very welcoming. Over the fire place was a shelf on which stood a variety of small silver framed black and white photographs of people, none of whom he recognised. Alongside them on the shelf was an attractive antique clock with hands and Roman numerals set behind a glass front. Ben then spoke to him. "Me misses name is Dora, and I be Ben" he said. " Ben Boswell of the Boswell's horse and donkey fairground folk I worked up at the Donkey lane years back and I kept ponies too". Terry was now sat at the table staring out at the large coloured landscape pictures which hung on all the patterned papered walls. All of these were of Gypsy encampments of long long ago,centuries long gone. Ben Boswell saw Terry's looks and remarked, "Oh they be my peoples long ago on the commons" he said. Then he said"I asked you a question sir, what be your name?". This time Terry answered him "Oh im so sorry Ben, I was taken back by your lovely room here, for its so different to what im used to". "My name, its Terry Hewes and my ancestors were Romani too" he said. Just then Mrs Boswell returned to the table with a mug of tea in her hand and said "Yes I could see you were a Hughes lad". Then as she offered him a drink she said "Here's you cuppa and some grub, get that down you young man". As she then placed some rolls on a dish in front of them both. Terry had taken the hot beverage from her and thanked her. He said, "this is very good of you Mrs Boswell". She smiled at him, then she handed her husband his drink, he took it from her hurriedly and drank it straight away despite it being very hot. Then he got up from his seat and went to his coat which he had previously hung on the door and took out the bottle of ale and placed it firmly on the middle of the table. "Wel have a little tipple of this in a minute," he said. "I got this bottle from old Alfie Squires he done a deal with me early today at the dogs". "Its the best stuff, its got lot a barley malt and al cha ale in it"he said. Then he spoke directly at Terry. " Here have this ere lad it will put airs on your chest young man" he said and he laughed. When they had finished their meal later and Mrs Boswell had cleared the table. Ben turned to Terry and asked him " Would you like to stay tonight? my missus is making up a bed for you in the spare room". Terry replied "Thanks yes, I wasn't going to, but I am getting tired now". Looking at his wrist watch he read 21 hours and 40 minutes. Shortly after Mrs Boswell returned to the room and Ben spoke to her. "The lads staying the night" he said. She smiled and said, "yes I thought he would i will just make up the fire a bit and then perhaps we could play a few table games whilst we drink the ale". Her husband Ben smiled.

So it was that later the box with its many table games were brought out from the cupboard and the young Terry Hughes was introduced to the games of ludo,snakes and ladders, draughts and tiddly winks. Then Mrs Boswell showed Terry around to his room and the bath room and she gave him a night shirt and night hat. Later as Terry washed at the sink in the bathroom he heard the front door slam and Mrs Boswell voice exclaim"its our Ruby!". He heard the young woman's voice "Sorry im late ma, they had me clearing up at the centre". He wondered where the centre was and if he had seen her in the city or in his zone. Then there was a silence and he crossed the hall into the spare room. Then after removing all his clothes he climbed into the bed. He had chosen purposely not to wear the night clothes they'd left on the side of the chair he always slept in the nude.

That night Terry had little sleep his mind going over the days events. He was concerned that he had found himself in an area he was not familiar with, particularly so, after Brian's warnings. He was not prepared for this and knew it was illegal. He was totally unaware that such neighbourhoods existed. Hadn't Brian warned him not to go into such prohibited areas. He thought of the fact that there were no screens here either, neither on the streets or in the houses. He wondered about the Boswell's daughter and couldn't wait to meet her. After what seemed like hours, but in fact was minutes, he finally fell asleep. But during the night his sleep was somewhat disturbed by the sounds of machinery in the night sky and a loud siren bleeping.

When Terry woke it was early morning, he looked at his wrist watch which read 700 hours. The sun was shining into the small bedroom window. As he got himself together he looked around the room. The wall pictures here were markedly different from those in the main lounge. Each one with fancy writing script which he had never seen before. Each one with a reference to a biblical scripture reading. The writings however he recognised from his studies on the big screen of earlier times religious texts. He moved slowly from his bed sitting on the edge of the bed whilst dressing. He heard the sound of voices from the lounge and laughter. He finished dressing and made his way out of the room into the hall. He went into the small bathroom where he washed and then he made his way to the lounge. Mrs Boswell was the first to greet him there. Mrs Boswell said"Good morning young man,i hope that you had a pleasant sleep". He smiled and said "yes I did despite the noise outside, what was that all about?" he asked. Mrs Boswell replied "That's the authorities searching for folks who are out at night when they should be in their beds." Ben Boswell laughed at his wife's remark. Then he spoke "there's a lot going on hereabout that you wont know of and perhaps its best you don't". It was then that Terry's eyes met those of the attractive auburn haired beauty who sat at the table. Ben Boswell saw his gaze and spoke "This here's our daughter Ruby". Then Ben then spoke to Ruby "Ruby this here's Terry." Ruby nodded. Then Ben asked him "Terry, don't you think she's a stunner ?". At this comment from her father Ruby blushed. Ben Boswell spoke to Terry "Ruby works in the city, but she knows most of the folks in this area. She will show you around after youv eaten some breakfast Terry". Mrs Boswell then spoke"Yes your not going yet young man, cause we want you to see how real people live and work". Terry smiled. Then Mrs Boswell spoke to him again "Come sit at the table and have some bacon and eggs" she said. Terry then moved to the far side of the table and sat next to Ben Boswell. Then he listened whilst father, mother and daughter discussed family matters and events as he ate the meal which Mrs Boswell had placed before him. Then Ben Boswell spoke to him "Our Ruby here will show you around this morning Terry, that's if its OK and your not in any hurry to leave us?". Terry replied "no I haven't any appointments this week, apart from a meeting the end of the week, no ones expecting me" he said. "You ain't got a young lady then?" Mrs Boswell asked with a twinkle in her eye. "No" he answered as he looked across the table and noticed the look of pleasure in Ruby's eyes. He couldn't help but look at her and admire her for she was so attractive a real beauty.

CHAPTER THREE

WOOD PECKERS YARDS

THE BRICK MAKER GYPSY

My granfer was a brick maker
he worked the kilns and downs
life was hard amongst the shifts
working for a crown

The landed gentry owned the land
whilst the common people prayed
the Gypsies worked the pits and clay
all the land around

The vardos and the benders
the huts with wagons strong
the chavvies running through the mire
with sweet lavender growing wild

The hours were long in brickyards then
when families were close
the donkeys and the ponies
the bricks sailed from the coast
My granfer was a brick maker
his family owned the yards
red bricks to build the town
with sand pits closely by
they worked the kilns and clay pits then
with Gypsies standing by

Ray Wills

WALK IN HER SHADOWS

I want to walk in her shadows
i want to be within her heart
i want to be in her world
cant live without her forever
we cant live apart

I want to be with her daily
be with with her each night
i hold a candle for her

She lightened my darkness in the night
she walked away with my heart
she's my delight

I want to walk in her sunshine
hold the key to her train
want to walk there besides her
again and again

I want to hear all her stories
all her troubles and pain
about her childhoods rich laughter
all her memories again and again

I want to share all the good times
as well as the bad
sickness and heartache
happy or sad

I want to walk in her shadows
i want to be in her heart
together forever
till death do us part

Ray Wills

ROMANY ROOTS

He had travelled through
those Romany roots
where cultures and heartaches
were seldom foolproof

He'd walked o'er the footpaths
where thorns tagged your toes
where rabbits and foxgloves
bridled your clothes

He'd stumbled on wise folk
who'd been through the wars
when peace was a haven
and Truth was ones word

His clothes they were tattered
and his language was rich
he'd laid in the gutters
the sideways and ditch

The lore of his nation
was caste to the winds
where freedom was gifted
with Romany rings

Where the sun hit you blindly
each morning at dawn
where the heavens were open
and your ways were forlorn

The paths they had ventured
o'er valley and dale
with scent of the flower
and the rich golden smells

Where your fortune was told
through the wink of an eye
where fairgrounds were rolling
and spirits were high

Like days long ago
when the soil was so rich
they travelled their wagons
through mud and low ditch

Where heather and fern
stretched for many a mile
where the Romany roots
were a haven a while
where the man was renowned
for the good in his smile

Ray Wills

GYPSY TIMES

To walk upon the turvebury heath
with only the sod beneath my feet
to whittle the branch and whistle the blade
and to while away the hour
twixt runs of wide rivers Trent and Stour

To ride the vardo and wagon once again
with cousin Jack and cousin Jane
to hear the goldfinch birdsong once again
at sunset to sit around the fireside then

To sing our songs and talk the tales
of Gypsy life and Gypsy gal
to ride the ponies once again
to hold on tight to leather reins

Over the heather tracks
of sand and stone
the common rides
that we called home
The grass roots rides and Gypsy talk
the knives we sharpened and pegs we turned
the floral wreaths and linen lace
the silver kettle pans shone
come see your face
the children played in barefoot chase
the rabbit runs and village fetes

The starry nights and moonlight tales
the geese that flew across the miles
took one back for quite a while
to those guitar days that used to be
when chavvies sat on granfers knees

Ray Wills

ROMA MAN

He was a genuine Travelling Roma
horses were his life
he lived on the heath and commons
worked the land with his lovely buxom wife

He was one of the old school Gypsies
who rode the lanes and dells
his family lived in benders then
afore the masters tales

He was a genuine Roma
with heritage which went way back
'twas when they worked the brick yards
sacking on their backs

He was a genuine Roma
his sisters worked the fields
baskets full of lavender
lots of floral goods

His mother went a duckerin
knocking on folks doors
his aunt she read the tea leaves
scrubbed the masters great hall floors

His father was a brick maker
craftsman of the old
the chavvies ran the dog pack
were happy boys and girls

Ray Wills

It was around 1000 hours that morning when Ruby was finally alone with Terry and she plucked up the courage and spoke to him. She said,"Terry, my Dad said I was to show you around this morning, if its alright?.yes of course" he replied. He smiled at her as she led him out into the yard. Hen Ruby looked at him and spoke again "Terry Our people are hard working folk, if you like il take you to Woodpeckers yard now and you will get a better picture of things?". "Yes of course" he said and nodded in agreement. It was obvious to her that he was very pleased to be in her company. She walked ahead of him now and like a stray dog looking for a home he followed her,whilst admiring her neat attractive figure from a short distance behind. As she walked ahead of him in the strong rays of the bright mornings summer sunlight. Her clothes looked strange to him for she dressed so different from all the girls he knew and mixed with in the city zone who were all very formally dressed. However he had seen similarly dressed women on the old newsreels from earlier days on the screen. He saw that Ruby's auburn rich hair was high on her head and yet hung long and flowing over her shoulders. When close up to her he had noticed her distinctive light blue eyes, her full lips and her neckline. The thin cotton floral patterned dress she wore today was cut low just above her splendid breasts, showing some cleavage. Whilst her dress length stopped just above her knees, showing of her long slender legs,whilst her shoes were high heeled and slim fitting. Her waist was small and the curves of her body from behind was most attractive. As he watched her body's movements walking ahead of him it made him feel so good. All in all he thought that she was indeed very attractive young woman. He guessed her age to be around twenty and he found her most sexually attractive. He followed just behind her through the yard and then down the lane. As they walked she spoke to him about the surroundings whilst occasionally turning and smiling. She said, "You will find our people very easy to talk with Terry, il introduce you to a few, if there's an opportunity". He nodded. "Dad told me yesterday evening that your from Gypsy blood Terry"she said. "Yes I am" he nodded. Then she said "you'll see that our folk here are all Romany too!". "We've been here for generation since they the authorities,gorgas changed the laws, since when we wernt able to

28

travel the highways or live in caravans as we had done for centuries past". As they walked side by side she said "Many of our people then found these places and made them our own". "Youl see that these areas are prohibited for use by their city zone folks known as the zone people". She continued talking to him about the life there. She said "Due to the false stories they put out of these areas being without any safety or hygienic standards regulations". "They no doubt told the zone people in the cities that there's a strong likelihood of risk of disease hereabouts". "But we survived! despite their laws!". She continued talking to him at great length , telling him more about the people and their lives there. She said,"our people still work the bricks, the pots and such places like they've always done". As he listened to her Terry thought back to the history he'd been taught and watched on the screen. Of the potteries in the city, where once thousands lived in filth and disease.

Ruby caught his gaze, along with his pleasure of seeing and observing her up close. She was aware of his eyes focused upon her neckline cleavage and embarrassingly she tried to avert his eyes from hers. She continued to tell him more of the histories of the area. She said"We create the bricks, pots and work the coal in the mines here". "Where I am taking you now Terry, is where all the brick yards, the potteries and the coal mines are based" ."All of these places are deep underground all are well hidden from the prying eyes of the authorities". She said "But as far as the city zone people are concerned no one tells them and therefore they don't actually know that our folk still exist". "The town folk in cities and the like are not told of such areas and of our people and how we labour". " The authorities keep it secret as it helps them to keep their coffers rich". "For believe it or not, Coal is still used by them as a means to generate electricity for their clean air society".Terry listened attentively as she told him much of what he already knew and much that he did not know. She said,"Our people living here still use currency, as they have always used it and their wages are very low, but we get by." "You will see Terry that both our Men, our women and our children all work here in the manning woodpeckers yard". She smiled and continued to explain how thing were. "You will see that they the workers here wear the same thin blue cotton masks for protection from the fumes and the furnaces"she said. She smiled at him seeing his expressions of amazement. She continued to talk "Yes,these are exactly the same masks that people wore during times of the great plague many years ago,nothings changed here" she said.

Terry followed close to her, then when he was by her side he looked her in the eyes than asked her, "so they let you all live and work here and yet they conceal it from the masses of the people!he said?".Then he asked her "so how do they get away with that lie?". As she looked him in the eyes he felt his heart was racing fast.

Then she answered him "Yes that's right Terry and even if anyone said anything they'd deny it all, as a conspiracy" "And you know the consequences of that?" she asked, "You know what happens to any conspirators in the organisation,don't you Terry?",

Terry nodded for he of course more than most knew too well. For it was an area in which he had been trained to watch out for. He knew too well that the consequence of such things was that of that of death by injection. She was walking down hill now ahead of him into a steep slope and he followed her then walked faster and closer to be beside her. When he was close to her he once again smelt her body's sweet aroma. He knew that he had to stay close to her as the area where they were was dark now. He walked alongside her now aware of her beauty and they walked down the hill together side by side, into a deep basin. They were well below the ground level now. They carried on walking until they were in a large wide dark chasm. Here there were three large earth tunnels just ahead of them, each one carved out of the ground and each with a individual marking on their roof.

Then Ruby stopped walking and looked directly at him and then she spoke again. "These are the three areas where our people work Terry" she said. "These are the brickworks,the potteries and the coal pits". "There's lifts here which lead down to their faces below and that's where im taking you to now Terry". He said "Thanks Ruby". She said"OK follow me","We will go to the brickworks today Terry".

Then looked into his eyes and she asked him with a twinkle in her eyes, "Well Terry, are you up for it?" she said. It looked like a tease of sorts, he never responded at first, so she asked him again, "Are you up for it Terry?". He looked into her eyes and he knew that he was falling in love with her. He answered her "yes I am definitely up for it" he said and smiled. He had answered her as best he knew how. For now he was very interested and wanted to know more, much more. More of his new surroundings, more of its people and especially more of Ruby Boswell.

His thoughts were racing in his head now, he was desperately trying to put it all together. It was in many areas so contradictory from his own life's educational training he had received through the organisation. Just then a tall middle aged dark and rugged looking man approached them. The man greeted Ruby with a familiar smile and a firm handshake. Ruby spoke to him with some familiarity and pleasure. She smiled at him and then and said "Bert here's someone I would like you to meet". "This is Terry Hughes, he's a good friend of ours he's one of us Bert". Then she turned to Terry and said "this is Bert Rogers Terry". She looked at Bert intently and then she said to him "Bert i would like you to show Terry around."

Bert smiled at Terry and offered his hand to Terry. Terry shook his hand firmly. Though as he did so he noticed Bert's hand was very calloused, hard, very wet and was covered in red clay. Bert looked at Terry with some acknowledgement, but for some reason was wary of him too. Then he spoke " I'm the manager of these here brick works and ive been here running this place for nigh on thirty years" he said. "Its been in my family afore me for years" he said. Ruby smiled at Bert then she affectionately touched Terry's shoulder gently with her right hand and said "look I've got to go now Terry but I will see you later tonight at home OK". Terry nodded. Then she said "Bert here will look after you and show you around Terry then later on he will direct you back to our home Terry OK". Terry smiled at her and said "Yes, yes of course thanks Ruby, i will see you later then Ruby". He smiled at her again and for the first time he saw the small rose tattoo on the flesh at the base of her slender neck. He watched her walk all the way back up the hill, till she was out of sight. He thought to himself how delightful her figure was and how much he wished he knew her better. Then he turned to face Bert Rogers. Bert was still busy watching Ruby's walk too and Terry had the distinct feeling that he wasn't just one of her friends.

Terry turned to face Bert Rogers and asked him "Ruby said you could answer a lot of my questions Bert?". Bert replied "yes i try" he said and smiled to himself. Then Bert looked at Terry intently and said "I think its best if I tell you a bit about the place. Its been here for centuries, basically its not changed that much since its start". He continued talking "I'm told a group of Gypsies got together after the great division of labour when it was hard to find work". "It was a time when anyone regarded as a Gypsy was seen as trouble as vagrants, in those days many were imprisoned for failure to pay parking fines for stopping on the roadsides back then whole families were split up, people lost their livelihoods back then once they brought in the Act against the right to park on stopping places". He continued to tell Terry the history of the area. He said"The councils then were cutting back on official sites too". He continued telling Terry the history. He said "It was so im told, a terrible time and many suffered from all kinds of illnesses apart from the great plague".Terry listened to him attentively as Bert continued to relate the background to him. "Our people were branded trouble makers wherever they went". "Much of it due to the news papers of that time telling false stories and blaming travellers for all manner of ills". He continued telling Terry about the place."Well these families who knew a little about business knew of this area and came here to set up themselves into yards"Bert continued to tell Terry all the background. "All of the area then was under the old Woodpecker estate laws then which was itself in a poor state at that time. Jeremy Sandford the writer playright of Cathy Come Home was well known in housing in the area then".

Terry listened intensively to Bert Rogers and then he asked him. "Who were those original Gypsies and these families do you know Bert?"he asked. Bert answered Terry straight away "well yes we do know,because its been passed down for generations in our Says our old ways and in our traditional tales" he said. "They were the Boswell's,Rogers,Brixeys,Sherwood's and Hughes families".

Terry was pleased to hear that his ancestors the Hughes were mentioned as being involved in such an enterprise way back then. Though he always used the surname Hewes. As they walked down the tunnel then into the lift he could hear the sounds the noise of men physically working below. Then the air was suddenly very warm and thick with clay dust and he found it hard to breath.. Bert spoke "Were getting near the yard now, come follow me and you will see how we work". Terry followed him out of the lift and deep down into the brick yard and as he walked the air became thicker than ever with the clay dust. And then he saw the red and white glow of the hot kilns and saw the groups of men crouched down moulding the clay bricks with their bare hands. There was great movements of people, men women and children here. It was noisy, he saw all of the people here were nigh naked, the women too showing their naked breasts all rudely exposed to the air and with their upper body sweating. Many men and women were using barrows,some heaped up high with clay and others with bricks. They were all busy pushing and wheeling the wooden wheelbarrows all to and fro backwards and forwards over planking, around the hot burning kins. He could barely breath for he wasn't used to such hot humid environments and he coughed loudly. Bert heard him cough and noticed Terry's difficulty with breathing and said, "Yes its a bit hot here me lad, were used to it though". Then Bert gestured to Terry with his hand and said,"cmon follow me, we best go into the cabin" . Then he led Terry into a wooden shelter which was placed some ways away from the noise and heat. Then once inside they sat down on some wooden boxes then Bert said,"That's better lad","So now you see what conditions are like here!".

Just then a head appeared around the door of the shelter, it was a short man. wearing a cap and he called Bert aside. Bert disappeared from views for a short while, then he re emerged carrying a large wooden heavy crate full of what looked like small brown bottles. Bert saw Terry's surprised look and said," Don't worry lad, its just ale lad, its for the men, so they can quench their thirst with this,it helps them to cope with the heat". "Isn't that intoxicating liquor?" Terry asked. Bert saw his looks of displeasure and then he answered him" Yes it has its drawbacks, but it keeps them happy too, although sometimes they do get fight-able or amorous towards the gal's here". "So I have sacked a few in the past, but they often are readmitted under strict orders they behave" he said. "As you can see Terry, I have a large workforce of some

400 men here, plus women and children". "Some amongst them are great brick makers, though most are labourers and apprentice brick workers,some can earn a good wage and keep their families in good stead provided that they don't blow their wages". "In the old days were told that wages were paid out in the inns or back room of the chapels and churches" he said. "Many a man blew his wages on drink there and then, or paid most of his money for a privileged seat in the church". Bert took a bottle from the wooden crate then took the metal top off it and handed the bottle to Terry. Then he said "Drink lad it will get rid the cough and ease the throat". Terry took it off of him and he drank from it reluctantly. But was surprised how it eased his throat. Bert talked more in the little hut to Terry about the yard for quite a while. Explaining how life had been for his people and how the system which prevailed outside was corrupt. Terry listened intently but still had difficulty in understanding why this was happening. Why would the organisation cover up these truths and for so long. All the years and the thousands of people who had no doubt gone through the system. Terry found it difficult to accept this that the organisation which had trained and had educated him and provided him with a decent living. How could such an organisation be bad?. His mind was in turmoil, as he listened to Bert. Then he realised that time was getting on as he looked at his watch and saw that it was approaching 1700 hours and he needed to get back to the Boswell's. Bert saw Terry's look of concern and said "i will take you back up the lift then to Cold blow lane, lad". Terry thanked him for all his time and went with him back into the lift then they went on up to cold blow lane.

Ruby Boswell heard her name called someone was calling her "Ruby". She turned from her work looked up and saw one of the masters of the centre walking towards her. "What's the problem" she asked "Your wanted in the office" he said "OK" she said "il just put my cleaning gear away". "It doesn't matter about that just leave it, the head wants to see you now" he said. "OK" she said" im on my way". She wondered what the problem was, Surely it wasn't her work there had been no complaints from the members that she knew of. As she knocked on the office door she heard the asters voice "come in Ruby" he said. As she entered the room she was surprised to see that there were others there. Two senior stewards were with the head of the centre. "Take a seat" he said. She sat facing the head and the two stewards. The head spoke "there's no other way I can say this, but looks like your no longer required to work here". He said "Its continued its come to our attention that youv not been totally honest with your personal details". He then said. "There's been some valuables missing and as you know we took all employees DNA and as a result Its come to our attention that your a member of the vagrant group". She was astonished. "But ive been a loyal employee havnt I?" she said. The head replied "Yes but that's not the issue here, you know our rules" he said. "Please go and change out of your work uniform and hand it to your supervisor". "Your income will be forwarded and you are no longer an employee of the centre from today". Ruby began to cry, "ive been here 3 year now ive loved it here" she said. He said. "It was also brought to my attention that you have a tattoo" he said. "Yes" she said "its my choice". He smiled and said " other staff members noticed it when you were all in the showers together and you know the rules" he said. Ruby stood up and looked at the stewards. The master spoke again "these two gentlemen will see you off the premises your services are no longer required here" he said. Ruby ran from the office in tear's. She went back to her works room where she changed her clothes removing the blue uniform of the organisation and changing back into her dress. Then she handed her uniform in at the reception and left the centre. Once outside she ran through the streets crying.

Terry Hewes eventually made his way back to the Boswell's arriving just in time for the meal with the family. It was good to see the smoke of the pot on the roof and to hear the voice of Mrs Boswell. As he knocked on the door she opened it, it was good to see her with her heart warming smile. She was please to see him too and spoke. "So good to see you young man just in time for dinner, we eat late here," then she laughed.

That evening Terry sat at the Boswell's table and ate a hearty meal of chicken and chips. He had never tasted potatoes cooked in fat before, so this was also a new experience for him. It was totally against the basic healthy living principles of the regime he had been trained under. Mr Ben Boswell arrived later, he was once again in a state of intoxication. He'd been to the inn and played nine card brag along sides his old mates. He was in a good mood today though due to the drink and was not too drunk. He chatted a lot about the inn he had visited.

Then Ben Boswell turned to Terry and asked him"less about me, how was your day Terry?. "Did my daughter Ruby introduce ya to the mush at the yard?". "Yes" Terry replied. "She took me down to meet the brick yard manager, a Mr Bert Rogers, Ben". Ben Boswell's expression then changed and he looked really concerned, as if annoyed and he asked Terry "I hope he didn't upset you lad? I know he can be a bit insensitive at times". "No" Terry replied "he was very helpful, in fact, he told me lots of history of the place, yes he was very kind" he said. Ben turned his head around and he looked up at the mantle clock on the fireplace shelf and then said, "Our Ruby should be home soon, she's a good gal".Terry asked him "Where does Ruby work Ben? is it a nice place?". Ben looked at Terry straight into his eyes and said,"Yes, I do hear its a very respectable place". The he said "She takes her time coming home, as she takes the long ways around by Greenwich park,so she don't get them suspicious, im always worried the authorities will find out she's a traveller gal and take her in"." I hear of those who get caught out and they are taken and if their pretty they do use them". "But she dresses well,she doesn't over dress our Ruby!", "no fancy jewellery for her, like those gypsy forest girls of the past". "She's not too flash and cheap,she always takes care of her appearance" he smiled. By his look and his talk Terry could see that he was worried about his daughter and her situation. For he was trying to reassure himself. Terry had the distinct feeling that something wasn't right here though and Terry had these nagging doubts that Bert knew more than he was letting on. Bert then shouted out "Where are you missus?,you see any signs of our Ruby, out there?."he said.. His wife called back "I'm here" she called back "ive been over to Mrs Roberts to get some flour Ben as ive got to start on our Ruby's cake, for its her birthday tomorrow". Ben answered her, "Oh yes of course,what we getting her my luv?". She replied "You know, you ole fool, we decided that weeks ago and you made an arrangement your mate Sam at the Inn". "I hope you remember your picking it up later today?" she said. He answered her,"Yes ill be sure to get it,for I have ready paid money down from last weeks winnings at nine card brag". Mrs Boswell laughed,you and your card games"she said. "Yes I remember" he said "its a pretty silver necklace with her name in gold".Terry smiled "Sounds lovely" he said. "How old is Ruby?"he asked. Ben answered automatically "She's 21 and never been"..

But before Ben could finish his sentence his wife Mrs Boswell shouted out at him "and wel have none of that talk here Ben Boswell". "Sorry luv," he replied.

Just than the front door opened in the hall. Mrs Boswell called out "Is that you Ruby". Then her daughter called back,"yes mum."

Then they heard her footsteps, as she ran up the stairs.

"What's up here?" Ben asked. Mrs Boswell answered him "I dunno luv, something up" "il go up in a minute and see".

Then they heard the sound of sobbing. "Oh deary me, definitely something not right" said Mrs Boswell.

Shortly after Mrs Boswell left the room and made her way upstairs. Then they heard Ruby's voice and her mothers in deep discussion. It was awhile after that when Mrs Boswell came down and joined her husband and Terry at the table.

"She's really upset" she said.

"What is it?" Terry asked.

Mrs Boswell replied, "Its the works where she goes Ruby said they had someone steal stuff and they will be taking everyone's DNA now, as its law now and has been for a while".

"Oh dear, now they will be bound to find out she's Romany" Ben said. Then his wife responded " yes and she used the false name Cordell ever since she's been there its been a few years now". "I remember our Eddie my brother he told her about the place and that they were looking for a smart girl." she said. Then she turned to her husband and said " remember your brother Frank got that false ID card made up for her Ben". "Yes" he replied. "So what's she going to do now my luv?" he asked. It was obvious that Mrs Boswell was now very distressed as she raised her voice when she answered him "Well she's already received her wage in her accounts, collected it she shall not go back there now, its too risky, I expect she will take what's going down there at the Wood peckers yard now,all in all its a poor goings on my dears" she said.

CHAPTER FOUR

RUBY NIGHTS

NEIGHBOURHOOD SWEETHEART

She was the neighbourhood sweetheart
born on the wrong side of town
she was beautiful and gifted
the word went around

She was the neighbourhood sweetheart
born on the wrong side of town
she was the neighbourhood sweetheart
everyone knew her name it got around
her family so poor known by their name

She was the neighbourhood sweetheart
she grew up in the lanes
her clothes thin and tattered
handed down through the name

Her folks came from wagons
and sites with strange names
they sat around their fires at night
told stories the same

She was the neighbourhood sweetheart
sold flowers a few
she walked in the meadows
on the heath lands of Poole
She was beautiful and gifted
She told fortunes a few
to the Lords in the manors
and the children with no shoes

She was the neighbourhood sweetheart
she had cousins a few
she was fancied by gentlemen
poor men and fools

She was the neighbourhood sweetheart
married her name
cousins and kin folk
celebrated her fame

She was the neighbourhood sweetheart
she lived down the lane

Ray Wills

KISSES IN THE SHADOWS

Kisses in the shadows
memories long and gone
moments they'll remember
when their song has sung

Footsteps in the darkens
where no man has trod
candles flames a flickering
on his steps to bed

Long forsaken memories
stranded in the past
frozen speeches lost and found
floating in the cast

Kisses in the moonlight
underneath the stars
just one step to madness
Jupiter and Mars

Holding hands and whispers
looks that say i do
passages of time
when boats sailed out from Poole

Crafted words that hit you
when you read the lines
like psalms and aspiration's
gathered in lost time

Walks beneath the shadows
running on the shore
splash of waves to greet one
who could ask for more

The sun comes out to greet you
its warmth caress your soul
lost in paradise together
love oh how it shows

Steps out there together
in the world of shame
where traffic lights
are changing
ever bright and rains
Water pools of blessings
like puddles in the park
kisses in the shadows
and cuddles in the dark

Friends and old acquaintances
like folks out of he past
running through the meadows
o'er the leaves and grass

The rainbow shows its colour's
and the birds they soar and screech
whilst children dance and play
each day hastened by life's breeze

Ray Wills

When Mrs Boswell had cooked the dinner and served the plates on the table Ruby entered the room. She looked tired and her eyes were red and sore from her crying. She spoke "Sorry about earlier I was very upset"she said. She was now dressed informally, wearing a white woollen top,light blue jeans and leather sandals. She sat at the table across from Terry. She smiled at him and spoke "Good evening Terry, I hope you found the visit to the yard interesting". "Bert's a good man, he is very knowledgeable and knows all about brick making" she said. Terry was pleased to see her, though he saw her eyes were very red and sore from crying. He answered her "Yes thanks Ruby, I found it really interesting, thanks for arranging it all for me, though it sure was hot down there!". Mrs Boswell spoke to her husband "Cmon Dad, get stuck in, I didn't spend me time cooking for you to just look at it". Ben laughed and answered his wife, "As usual youv done us proud woman, the stew looks lovely dear." As Terry ate the meal he found that he was pleasantly surprised by its variety of tastes. It was so different from the meals he had back in the city zone from the computer chef. He turned to Mrs Boswell and asked her "Mrs Boswell this is lovely meal, can you tell me what you use to give it this taste?". She replied "Yes Terry its beef stew, it has all the vegetables from our communal allotments and ive added spices,salt, pepper and garlic to bring out the flavour". Terry had heard of these additives from the screen in his apartment and he knew these were prohibited as being contrary to the organisations health Acts enacted by the health safety and standards committee. He had however never tasted such meals which enriched it. He was pleasantly surprised how much he was enjoying the experience.

Later that evening after they had enjoyed their table games and went to their bedrooms Terry stretched out on the bed in his room. Then his mind went over the days events and the strangeness of it all. He had always believed in the organisation that the leaders who instructed him. And of course that the information on the screen was all correct and all was for his benefit. He believed that the organisation was always right with its rules and procedures. That the society had created a sound system of government based upon providing each of its members with a full healthy long and fulfilling life. A life where such things as illnesses, diseases, wars and poverty were of the past civilisations. The aim of each member was to improve their life, to attain a sound purpose and some were destined to greatness. The organisation provided each person the opportunity to attain that greatness. To travel to other countries was well in reach of all now, transport was quick. One could travel to Americas in a matter of hours now and visit the centres of excellence of each city zone. As he lay there he thought that these people here who were obviously outsiders of the standards of society. Then he thought of those like him who were brought up in the cities and wider world. Whilst these people here the Gypsy traveller kin, were obviously happy. Despite their poor circumstances, poverty and way of life. They appeared to be much happier than his colleagues, friends and acquaintances he had known in the numerous zones of the cities and of the new world order. They seemed contented despite living in squalid conditions of polluted smoke filled skies and their diets full of junk foods and additives. He had tasted the tea which they the Boswell's consumed so many cups of each day and night. Each cup was of sweet sugar no doubt. Though all of these were as he knew extremely bad for ones general health. He felt that they did however provide pleasures of tastes which he had never passed into his mouth during his lifetime and was to him a nice pleasant experience.

He had seen that the workers in the yards were working in intolerable conditions and dangerous risky practices. These were long outlawed in a decent society. For even their women and children endured these conditions. The ale they consumed in large quantities in their work places, in the inns and in their homes was no doubt full of alcohol and additives. These were poisons which caused euphoria and ultimately addiction. Along with the likelihood of acts of violence, or sexual assaults, not withstanding their effects on their own liver and kidneys. Though he having drank the ale himself at the yard and at the Boswell's now had surprisingly found it most enjoyable. Though bitter in taste it gave him a warm glow inside and feeling of well being and made social discourse much more pleasurable. He thought of how the screen and his computer system provided him with such complexity. Even his emotions and desires were controlled through it. For its system provided a particular section where one could evaluate ones future.

He knew that in his modern world, there was little differences between man and woman in life. Women wore the same clothes and filled the same positions in work and leisure. He was approaching the age where he was expected to choose a life partner whether man or woman. His computer system as he discovered could provide access to a data base of each member of society within his age range for to choose such a life partner. He was able with others to access pictures of each individual based on suitability and geared to his own needs. Each persons profile showed a nude picture of their body scanned from head to feet showing in great detail their beauty or ugliness. Here their sexual attractiveness was defined. In the case of females their breasts, vagina, buttocks and even pubic hair or lack of were shown in great depth and intimate detail. As with the male, his genital region was again fully exposed in detail along with his hairs, beard or otherwise. Along with frontal and rear shots in face. In fact every angle of their body. Alongside this was access to the persons voice.

The details of all their own likes,dislikes and their DNA and origin of ethnicity. Along with their favourite music, art works, poem or film. Terry had spent considerable time in recent months going through the numerous individuals data to make his decision and yet he had still not decided which one to select. Despite choosing his partner for life the person he chose had to agree to him as their particular choice, too often such a process took months if not years. Although the computer did monitor and assist throughout. Meeting Ruby outside this system however had thrown him completely off track. For his emotions were somewhat thrown into an area which he was totally unprepared for. Her femininity and her very aroma of perfume and her attractiveness was something in which he had not encountered before. Despite the organisation providing opportunities within the city zones to familiarise themselves with the opposite sex in places of desire. Such places were in easy access where female and male custodians offered sexual services. He had used these himself on numerous times. In the old systems these were known as brothels, but in the order they were rooms of satisfaction. All had strict medical guidelines and use of condoms and contraceptive measures. Of course the population of the present age had diminished and was reduced considerably. Mainly due to few opposite sex partnerships. There were now as many same sex partnerships as opposite sex partnerships. Thereby reducing the population so that over the centuries the number of births had been reduced by millions. There were no more large families of earlier times with 6 or more offspring. One or two offspring's was the norm now. Plus male and male partners and female and females were able to foster a child and females were to play a less sexual role specifically for childbirth. Now they enjoyed a full sexual life pleasures as they wanted without fear of pregnancy. He thought to himself it must have been terrible in those very early days for pregnant young ladies with no life partner.

As he lay there he heard the ticking of the large hall clock. Which the Boswell's called grandfather. Again this was something new to him too as all was digital within the present age. The Boswell's appeared to have these clocks everywhere. He was tired now and yet his mind was full of questions and puzzles. Much of it didn't make sense to him any more. There were so many contradictions racing through his mind. As he lay there he heard sobbing coming from down the hall and he knew it was Ruby crying in her room. He got up from his bed and made his way into the hall, he heard the sobbing coming from the room at the end of the corridor. He stepped quietly till he was standing outside her door. He stood there for a while then the sobbing continued within the room and he knocked gently on the door and he whispered the question, " Are you OK Ruby?" he asked. Then there was silence which seemed to last forever, then eventually in the quietness she answered him, "sorry I disturbed you Terry love, you can come in if you like I am dressed and respectable". Then he heard her giggle. He entered Ruby's bedroom, quietly closing the door behind him. He saw that she was sat upon her bed facing him and smiling at him through her tears. The room was nearly in complete darkness except for the light flickering of the small candle on her side board. She moved aside on her double bed making a space for him next to her and she said"come sit here besides me Terry", "I don't bite!". He moved to the bed and sat on the edge of the bed next to her. He once again smelt the sweetness of her body's perfume. As he sat close to her and he became used to the dim flickering light of the candle in the darkness. He could now see that she was wearing a thin, light blue floral patterned cotton nightdress with pretty lace edging. It was a dress which showed off her fine figure being nicely cut with a low neckline and it ran down to just below her knees. It didn't take much for him to realise or to be aware that she was completely naked beneath the nightdress. For as she had moved on the bed for him to sit next to her he saw the rise and fall movements of her naked breasts and he was aroused. He whispered"Are you alright now Ruby?" he asked " yes" she answered."I feel a whole lot better now, especially as your sat here besides me". She smiled at him then she looked into his eyes and placed her hands on his and stroked them both gently with her fingers. He felt her body move up close against his as she snuggled into him. Then she moved her face close to his and looked deeply into his eyes. Then their lips met and he tasted her and his hands were on her and he was embracing her. His hands hurriedly undid the small buttons of her nightdress and saw and he felt the pleasure of her firm naked flesh of her breasts for the first time and saw the beauty of her nakedness. As he took and held her firm breasts in his hands his fingers caressed her nipples. Swiftly he removed her nightdress and he saw her naked body. She laid back down delightfully stretched herself out on the bed. He kissed all of her body passionately and she felt his mouth and tongue pleasuring her. He discovered for the very first time the joy and sweet taste of her most intimate flesh. Then he felt her feminine hands upon him. She undid his jeans and he felt the pleasure of her soft fingers caressing his erect manhood. Then they were both naked. They awoke to the morning to the beautiful sounds of chorus of the goldfinch outside on the heath.

CHAPTER FIVE

GOING STEADY

LONG NIGHTS AND NEW DAYS

His thoughts were of her in the morning light
he blew out the candle diminished the night
the daylight was dawning and the sky was so blue
only the shadows left him with a love so true

The night-time dreams bothered him no more
with their imagery visions and their sad eyed blues
the thoughts came in and the tears fell free
he kissed her memory and the roaring seas

The heartaches were over and the days gone by
today's joys were awakening amidst the new found sighs
the stars had twinkled once now they lost their glow
he whispered prayers then of so long ago

The night had gone and the new day was here
he glanced at the time and drank his beer
his glass half empty some say half full
he knew he'd loved her in a strange world so cruel

Like the beer he tasted and the joys he knew
in a life of gambling and common fools
the haunts of taverns and their ladies so free
with their offers aplenty and and their love so free

He dressed and gathered his thoughts anew
put on a smile and his faded shoes
he put on a shirt of rich attire
put on those jeans his heart afire

He heard a clock struck seven and cars passed by
he saw the neighbours all go by
how time doth fly

The children's voices he heard anew
and the merry band played
a tune on the radio of sad soft blues

He listened to the news
on the screen and sighed
the past was just another war and
another royal bride

Ray Wills

In the morning at the breakfast table Terry and Ruby had informed Ruby's parents that they were an item. That they were now "going out, or going steady ". It was a term that Ruby used and that which her parents were both familiar with and was much to their delight. "How wonderful!" Mrs Boswell remarked whilst Ben smiled that "knowing look" of his and said that"i knew all along" without them telling him. For as he said " it was obvious to a blind man". Then Mrs Boswell spoke,"Now listen up, this is important, today is special, for its our Ruby's birthday today she's 21 years". Then she said "Just think twenty one years ago you were born Ruby". "Old Mrs Dunker-in delivered you, as we had our babies at home then and we still do,cant beat the old ways"she said. " It was in the early hours and id been in labour for eternity". Ben laughed when she said that and then he said "you bant telling the truth there woman as it twere just a few hours woman". They all laughed, then Mrs Boswell said " Happy birthday me girl here's your present from Dad and I, we hope you like it". She handed Ruby the red gift box in great anticipation. Then Ben spoke " Well open it then Ruby girl!". Then Terry said " yes, happy birthday Ruby, il get you something nice when im next in the city my love".

Ruby held the small gift box her mother had given her in her hands. Then she slowly undid the wrapping and opened the small package and then its red box box within. When she saw the necklace inside she was so pleased, her eyes lit up and she exclaimed "Ho, Mum, Dad, you shouldn't have, its lovely, it must have cost you a fortune". Then her father said "only a months beer money" and he laughed. Ruby said "its lovely" and she gave them both big hugs. "Put it on then Ruby" Terry said "here let me help you Ruby".Terry took the necklace from her and placed it around her neck, then clipping the clasp together behind her neck he said "its really nice, it really suits you Ruby." As he hung it around her neck he once again saw the tattoo there. It was of a red rose in bloom, dainty and well drawn.

Later that day Terry went with Ruby, down to the yard for her to sign on with Bert. She was to assist him in his office with coping with any problems which might crop up amongst the workers in the future. She arranged with Bert that she would start work there the following week. Over the next few days Terry and Ruby were constantly in one another's company. Terry had moved into Ruby's bedroom now and their long intimate nights together in her double duck down feathered bed continued and were full of passion. As Terry further discovered the most intimate delights of her body and Ruby felt loved as never before. Over the next few days Terry and Ruby also spent many long hours talking together about life and their future together. Then Terry told her "I will have to leave on Friday Ruby, as ive an appointment with the head of zone 8 to discuss my future role in the organisations forum". He knew deep down that things wouldn't be the same it wouldn't be easy. Particularly now that he had broken many of the

organisations rules, practices and procedures. He now had many doubts and also had a nagging thought in the back of his mind that he was being constantly watched,even here at the Boswell's. Plus the fact that despite being in love for the first time, (an experience he hadn't known before)he was now developing a sore throat and a persistent cough for the first time in his life. He wondered if he had picked up a germ from the yard. Or was it the love making germ that the computer screen had warned him against if ever he should get involved in any illicit practices outside of the organisations wonderful rules of protection.

When Friday morning arrived Terry said his goodbyes to Ruby and her parents the Boswell's and he set off for the city. His chosen route took him through Sanford walk where once the liberal Jeremy Sandford co operative museum stood. He eventually made his way into Greenwich and noticed immediately how quiet it was and how clean the air was. He passed by a few people who were busy looking at the organisations landmarks and the proud standard buildings. Then his watch bleeped, he slipped the micro phone out and put it to his ear. A familiar male voice spoke, "you have an appointment at 1600 hours today with the sole leader" . He answered. " yes I know sir, thanks for reminding me". Then there was a humming noise and the phone went dead. He took the micro phone from his ear and slid it back into his wrist watch and went on his way. It was once again a lovely day with a clear blue sky. It was all thanks to the organisation. He passed another zone with its all too familiar landscape and made his way to his own more familiar home zone. Then he saw the sign ahead it bleeped out "you are entering zone 8, this is zone 8". Here there was another large community screen ahead showing his location in greater detail. He made his way back to his small apartment and was so relieved to see his own entrance smell the honeysuckle and hear the goldfinch song.

Later that day after he'd rested Terry logged into his own screen in his apartment and selected his meal from the daily menu on the computer grid. Then he took the hot plate and sat at his table and as he ate he was surprised how tasteless the meal was compared to those he'd eaten at the Boswell's. Then after he'd eaten he cleared the table. Then at 1600 hours he logged into his screen. He was surprised that it took its time to register and then when it did it questioned him. The voice on the screen said "good afternoon, what service are you requesting Terry Hewes? " he answered, "appointments". The computer answered "I'm sorry your information details are not registered, please reboot". Terry was surprised as this had not happened previously, but he did as he was asked, he turned the screen off then shortly afterwards switched it back on again. This time he was successful,the screen lit up and then he saw the master of the 8 zone on the screen. The master spoke, "good afternoon Terry Hewes welcome to today's session". Then he said "The organisation wish to thank you for your work and after careful study of the material you provided in the last session,we would like you to pay us a personal visit to headquarters tomorrow at 1000 hours". "This will give you an opportunity to discuss your needs with us and for us to state our requirements on the data required for the future". Terry was surprised by the request to attend a meeting so soon,which would give him very little time to prepare. However he knew that one did not question the organisations requests and he answered "Thank you master for your request,yes I will attend tomorrow with my report and data as requested". The computer made a musical sound then it closed down. Terry pressed the blue button on the monitor keyboard and the programme kicked back in once more. A voice asked "what programme are you requestioning Terry Hewes?". He answered "Life partner." There was a click then the new page came up on the screen. He typed into the search panel the words in capital letters RUBY CORDELL along with her date of birth details then her country of origin. Then a new page appeared before him on the screen with profile pictures of around a dozen women. He looked through them then saw Ruby's picture and pressed the green go button next to it. The computer made a lot of noise as it went through the process followed by a new page which came up on the screen. This was now flashing words in bold capitals along with the voice. "PROHIBITED. THIS AREA IS CONFIDENTIAL OUT OF BOUNDS. YOUR ACCESS IS DENIED". Then the computer closed, switching itself off automatically

CHAPTER SIX

WERE WATCHING OVER YOU

HIDDEN AGENDAS

I was told they had their own hidden agenda
with words of truth and lies
all crafted in their secret code
like terrorists and spies

There were thoughts to make one listen
and sounds that no one heard
but they sold them to the lambs and sheep
like slaughters to the wolves

The drifting congregations
were heralded and free
with secret words of innocence
lost in a lovers plea

The walls were thick with common trust
and music filled the air
like sacred passages of rhyme
and soulful passing airs

No matter of their promises
the truth was plain to see
crafted in the words of truth
and sold as liberty

The fowl of the air they guided me
and the victor set the scene
within the walls of consequence
and landed gentry scenes

There was laughter around the tables
it echoed across the plains
till the master of the guided truths
stood out all alone again

Ray Wills

WHY DOES THE CAGED BIRD SING

Why does the caged bird sing his song
of freedom each spring day
why does the infant play
before he attends school today

Why does the poet write
and the song smiths perform
In winter calls and snowflakes fall

Why does the caged bird sing
his songs of freedom each and every spring
Why does the prisoner pray
for freedom inside the walls
why do the oppressed campaign
for justice and oppose the dictators reign

Why does the hedgehog sleep in leaves
beneath the wagon vardo lodge
close to the yog with embers bright
in the darkest hour of the night
why does the caged bird sing its melodies
its songs of freedom in the breeze

Ray Wills

For the rest of the day Terry worked on his report ready for tomorrows meeting. Though he did do a search on the screen on the Boswell's family. The result of which was that the Boswell's were for centuries one of England's largest and most important Gypsy families. He read that the Boswell clan were a large extended family of Travellers and in old Nottinghamshire dialect the word bos'll was used as a term for Travellers and Romanies in general.

He drifted in and out of thoughts for his mind was full of concern over his attempt to access Ruby's profile. Even by the evening he couldn't relax for thinking about it and what it meant. That night in bed his sleep was disturbed numerous times by strange dreams. At one time he had to get up and get himself a drink and spend a few minutes thinking through the dreams and trying to resolve his dilemma. He knew he would be unable to access Ruby's profile again. It was foolish to attempt to try to and may well effect his future position within the organisation. He had to hope that it wasn't serious though no doubt it would greatly question his future with Ruby. There were many thoughts going through his head. Such as could Ruby be involved with a underground terrorist body or be under suspicion by the organisation or involved in crime. It had put his whole relationship in future with Ruby under a great deal of concern and in jeopardy. He eventually got off to sleep in the early hours and when he did awake it was 800 hours.

Terry left that day for his meeting with the grand master of the organisation with a great deal of apprehension. He crossed the city from zone 8 through 12 and then crossed to the multi complex building in room 10 of the central zone. He had worked on the Report over some 12 weeks now and felt that he had put together a sound system of future possibilities. His report covered the future levels of growth that he envisaged substantially should the organisation follow through his suggestions. It covered all aspects of the young peoples growth into maturity. No longer were they to be grounded in certain aspects of the past. Such as their intuitive need to take part with their peers in unnecessary time wasting activities. But now they would be able to fully concentrate to channel their energies into more constructive ways and means. As to further the organisations sound practices. He had aimed to replace their fantasy and preoccupation with idle activities,which in the past times was called play along with the foolish imaginations of their ancestral backgrounds. Their time would be better spent in positive creativities of educational improvements. The gymnasiums of the present would be further extended into academias of health and fitness. Based on the implementations of further mandatory vaccine programmes which were titanically implemented during he great plague. His was to prevent any germs entering their bodies. The foods they consumed daily would be further enhanced with chemicals to provide supplements of growth of brain and Altair blood advancement. He had studied all the details from the organisations data bases and also looked at the rate of ageism The present average ages of man n woman could be strengthened from its present 120 years to 160 years. The period of youth namely from 0 to 18 could be substantially reduced from 0 to 10 year. Therefore adulthood would be sooner in their life cycle rather than later. Thus in this way adult life would be fundamentally improved and able to provide more industrious intelligence rather than in idle day dreaming. As he made his way into the main street zone he had growing doubts on his own sincerity. Although he had completed the report he had doubts which troubled him. He knew what was expected of him. He knew that he would most likely be rewarded with a higher rank a new level within the organisation and thus gain financial security. But inwardly he felt troubled,troubled by his involvement with Ruby and fear that this involvement could put him at risk too. There was also the disturbing thoughts that the organisation although no doubt sound had a number of defects. He had experiences at the Boswell's home and at the yard things which put a new slant on the matter. All which troubled and disturbed him for he had doubts now that the organisation had misled the people. Even his data bank he thought could be too extreme and showed them in itself that there were problems within our new order. Terry wondered what the master would look like and would say to him. This was the first time he had been summoned to the central meeting rooms. As he entered the main reception area he was met by two stewards. Both of whom were dressed in the familiar light blue long jackets of the organisation. It was obvious that they were expecting him. He showed them his card and the number on his wristwatch. They screened him with their scanner then their usual arms greeting and he was escorted to a white room with red cushions and told to wait. Shortly after he heard the footsteps in the hall coming towards him. The master greeted him with a friendly smile and the usual cross arms salute then led him into a small office. The room was bare too and its wall were white with no pictures and the room had no furnishings apart from two large wooden chairs with the familiar dark red cushions. "Seat Terry" he said. He was a rather short man with a good head of hair, he was well tanned and looked liked he used the gym regularly. He spoke to Terry "Terry we have watched you and observed your work and progress with much interest". "We have up to now been extremely pleased with your progress and hope that it will continue likewise in future". Terry answered him "thank you master I have enjoyed my studies and the work and hope too that I will continue to please the organisation". The master asked him "Now Terry have you brought your report?".Terry replied "yes master" and he reached into his coat picket and handed the document to the master. "Thank you Terry I will read this with much interest" he said. Then he said "I hope that we can consider its recommendation and put your projections and suggestions into effect, the organisations committee of progress will get back to you on the screen within the next few days Terry". He looked intently at Terry then he asked him "Have you any questions or concerns?". Terry answered " no thank you master I hope that you will enjoy the read and I look forward to the committees response". The master then spoke again "Before you go, there's something I wish to know Terry?, can you tell me on your visit to Brian Delaux recently why you chose to stay there overnight?."You did stay overnight didn't you ?" he asked. Terry was surprised at this question for it wasn't what he was expecting and completely threw him. Then he replied"No I didn't sir". The master smiled, then said "Well Terry, thank you for attending today we will be in touch again if your needed". Terry was surprised at the short interview session and its abrupt end he was expecting a more intensive meeting, Then they exchanged the usual cross armed salute greeting and Terry made his way back to the reception. Where the two stewards scanned him once again. Then they escorted him out into the warm sunshine. Where once again they exchanged the usual cross arms salutations. Then Terry was by himself out on the street. He looked at his watch it read 1105 hours. He heard its familiar bleep and slid the micro phone out of the watch placed it in his ear and a voice said "thank you for your participation, the committee will be in touch within three days" then it bleeped and was quiet. He slid the micro phone back into the wrist watch on his wrist and he began his long walk home. As he walked the city zone he felt upset for he knew that something wasn't right. The master was very strange, there was little depth to the meeting. It was as if he wasn't there to talk about his report at all and the question about staying overnight at Brian's wasn't what he had quite expected and he wondered what was that about. The master didn't push him about where he had slept overnight. It was as if they knew that he had entered the forbidden zone. He remembered that Brian had warned him of the danger of entering the prohibited zones. He wonderer how much the organisation knew and if they had been watching him there in the forbidden area. He wondered what was the remark by the master about watching him. Did it mean literally watching his movements and not his career progress and the high standard of his work.

Over the next few days Terry relaxed at home. Apart from visiting his favourite parkland at Greenwich. He was waiting for the message from the organisations committee. But for some reason it never came within the allocated times. He went onto the screen every day, awaiting a message and hoping, but none arrived. He began to worry and wondered if they were checking up on him. He considered contacting Brian, but decided that maybe it wouldn't be good if they were watching him. He knew the organisation had access to all messages on the phone or on the screen. He knew it only right that they did so to ensure the safety of the people. The people always were their top priority and they encouraged each individual to become the best they could be. No longer were people used in factories and places of stress. They had since the great plague been encouraged to work from home. So that's how it was as the years went by and the organisation evolved. As was forecast by many old politicians of the past. As being in the great NEW WORLD ORDER. After a week he decided that he would contact

Brian and ask if he could visit. When he eventually phoned Brian. Brian told him that he wondered if he was OK as he had not heard from him since his last visit. They talked for a few minutes then they arranged for Terry's visit the following day.

CHAPTER SEVEN

AT THE MANSIONS BIRD ZONE

GOLDFINCH AND MINERS DAYS

The goldfinch sang upon the heath
and the minor in its cage
the canary song of yesterday
like an idol on parade

The thistles grew upon the downs
and the poor boy sang its tunes
the days of daisies on the green
and the bosom dairy maids

The sweet sounds of the cuckoo bird
as it flew from Stoborogh green
where meadows kissed the foxgloves buds
and the rivers set the scene

Where blackbirds thrilled its melodies
and the rabbits ran the downs
where idle men with idle talk
all bet on half a crown

The Gypsy vardos passed you by
and the ukuleles played
the young gal's danced upon the green
and the young men had it made

The sun shone through the clouds of spring
and the chaffinch flew away
where springtime buds were rich in scent
and the wise men went to pray

The miner bird does sing its song
like so beautiful in tone
whilst children loved its melody
and sang their ways back home

Through the crossways rich
in thorn and briar's
and the babies slept in peace
where Gypsies roamed upon the downs
and the good Lord kept the peace

Ray Wills

GOLDFINCH DAYS

He was raised at the Mannings
where the goldfinch did sing
in long summer months
in the thistles from the dawn of each spring
Where the orchards was rich
in pear trees and fall
where pigs were once kept
amidst the good and rich soil

He ran with the dogs
and gave chase to the packs
schooldays at Branksome
and times playing jacks

In wartime he travelled out to the East
he drove generals and captains
with his Dorset rich speech

On returning to England
he drove for a while
from the dockside's of Weymouth
to the New Forest wilds

He loved to play darts
and shove halfpenny too
spending days on the farm
and night out at Poole

His stories were rich
in tone and in depth
with his humorist anecdotes
and his lengthy Odette
his dart throwing visions
and quick witted speech

Though the birds were his fancy
with feathers all set
pigeons and doves
with canaries his best
His stories he told
to children in rhymes
once upon a time
when the bees drank the wine

Hel be remembered
as the storyteller of the heath
with his own unique brand of humour
and his rich dialect speech

Every time you hear
a Johnny Cash song
or a child's happy laugh
you l see his smile

and his unique country ways
it l all come back
not forgotten
in young springtime
of goldfinch days

Ray Wills

When Terry woke up the following morning it was to the sound of thunder. It had rained heavy all night and it had kept him awake off and on for most of the night. He looked at his watch it read 700 hours. After toiletry and then a breakfast of oatmeal and milk he made preparations for his visit to Brian's. They had agreed any time after 1000 hours and that he would stay for lunch. Once he had checked on the screen to make sure all was well, he packed a few items in his case to show Brian. Then he looked out of the window and was relieved the rain had stopped and the sky was clearing. He dressed casually, jeans and sweater but with long raincoat he wasn't taking any chances. He didn't want to catch any germs. His throat was still sore and he now had a nasal drip and diarrhoea, such things he had never known. He wondered if he had contacted some disease from the Boswell's particularly from Ruby. He knew so little about her and had now doubts about her own fidelity. He thought back to when she had introduced him to Bert at the Yard. Looking back he thought that they seemed to know each other too well,far too well.

Then he made his way outside where the air was warm and it smelt of honeysuckle from his small garden wall. The goldfinch were singing as usual. He hurriedly made his way through the city zone, the traffic was heavy in the sky above today. When he eventually arrived at the birds zone it was just before 1000 hours. He saw Brian standing outside his apartment and beckoning him. Brian greeted him with the usual cross arms salutation and said "Its great to see you matey, come through Terry". Terry followed him into the apartment. He smelt the coffee being percolated its roast beans aroma was such a pleasant welcoming smell, They sat together in silence for a while whilst drinking the hot coffee. Then Terry spoke " I havnt been in touch for a number of reasons, I was preparing my report for the organisation" he said. "They had only given me a day to complete it" he said."Then I had to or was instructed to attend a meeting with the master at the organisation headquarters so it was all a rush". Brian nodded and replied "oh so now youv actually met the grand master, what was your impression of him and tell me how did it go?" he asked "Well Brian,it wasn't quite like I had expected he replied "for he was completely different than I had imagined and though he excepted my report,then he informed me that the committee would be in touch with me within three days". "But then nothing happened Brian he said" he said. "In fact I waited three days, then I hung on a few more days just in case". "That's why I didn't get back to you Brian". Brian nodded then he spoke "so how was it, what did they say about your ideas then Terry? "Are they accepting your recommendations Terry?" he asked. Terry answered "I don't know Brian" "I still have not heard anything" Brian said "Oh dear,that's not good and so how was your talk with the grand master Terry?" Terry answered him " well he actually said very little and I wasn't there for long Brian, in fact I was quite disappointed he was very different,different ", Brian asked him," in what way was he different Terry"?, "What do you mean different Terry?". Terry answered,"Well he didn't ask me any questions I expected him to Brian,that is then at the end he did ask me one question that totally threw me". Brian acknowledged Terry's remarks and nodded with some understanding and said "Yes I do understand Terry I know he can be very discreet at times and also very probing". "So no doubt he asked you if you had stayed here overnight I expect?". Terry was very surprised by Brian's question, "yes Brian,how did you know that Brian?" he asked. Brian replied"Well I expected that would be asked at sometime,they have to check out to see if your choosing a life partner without going through their usual choosing a partner programme procedures ". Terry looked at Brian with complete astonishment and then asked him "So your saying that he was checking out our relationship?" he said. Brian answered him "yes maybe, or perhaps he knows something else?". Terry responded "Like what?" he asked. Brian answered "I don't know Terry, maybe because of your progress they have to be extra careful,did you hear of anything else when they were checking out your Romany ancestry Terry?" he asked. Terry answered him"No I didn't, but I know that as far as the organisation is concerned that ethnic group no longer exists".Brian spoke "So is that what they told you Terry?"Brian asked. Terry answered him " Yes, yes in my earlier training they said that those vagrants known as Egyptians were near nigh exterminated along with those counterfeit false ones claiming to be Gypsite also were hung and the group namely Roma were also taken off the roads centuries ago and were no longer a threat to our organisation". Brian said "Oh so that's what they told you?". Terry replied. "yes that's what they said Brian". Brian asked him "And you believed it?" "well yes of course" Terry answered. Brian asked him "Did they tell you that gypsies often were given a choice of hanging or slavery?" Terry replied,"no I never knew that Brian". Brian spoke "well they were Terry and many of those thousands chose to be slaves". Brian asked him "Did they ever mention slavery at all Terry?. Terry said "no but I read it on the screen Brian that those were being mainly black Caribbean ethic races and it was outlawed" . "So did you see about Barbados?" he asked . Terry said "no, like what?"he asked. Brian replied"Well you should have my friend, because that's where thousands of Gypsies were put to work on plantations". "Amongst them were the young busty gypsy girls who were sold fortunes for the highest prices on the blocks". "Any way Terry my young friend, just be extra careful as your in a good position and you don't want to ruin your promotional chances when your so in demand"he said. Then Brian reached out and patted Terry on the shoulder and said"your a good lad". Terry smiled and said "Thanks my friend", Then Brian spoke " Look Terry,I've ordered a nice meal on the screen i thought wed eat here and go into my library after".Terry replied," You have another Library here then too besides this one, I didn't know you had access to a separate library Brian?. "Are they micro chip data bases?"he asked. Brian answered,"Yes ive a wide ranged collection of musicals I want you to listen to and get your input Terry". Terry said,"Sounds good Brian, it sounds like youv been busy too".

They sat for lunch at midday then later relaxed in the separate music library. Terry listened to Brian's orchestral arrangement of the classics. He sure had been busy he thought. For he had never heard nothing like the sounds Brian had created. It was like nothing he had heard before. It reminded him of the goldfinches dawn chorus he heard in the early spring outside his window on the heath. It was a medley familiar to him in a strange sort of way, a sort of goldfinch canary rhapsody. "Amazing" he said "its amazing Brian". Brian caught his compliment and said "Yes I think ive got something fantastic", "I just hope the organisation will appreciate my work". Terry answered "I'm sure they will Brian he said. Then he said "oh yes that reminds me Brian I have some work in my case id like your views on". He took the case from his coat pocket laying nearby and handed it to Brian and said "Il leave it with you and collect next time I visit if that's OK Brian". "Yes of course il be glad to look it over Terry" he said "and by the way Terry, when you left on your last visit, did you have any trouble getting back to the city? He asked "Because I know there's often some strange folks across the way who sometimes cross the line". Terry looked at Brian then said "no I found the way back like you said. I kept to the street and didn't falter" he lied. "That's good Terry one never knows whose out there." Terry spoke " Il be going in a minute Brian as I want to get home before dark". Brian said"I don't blame you Terry just don't take too long before your next visit". Terry said "No I wont, thanks for everything Brian, especially the meal, I enjoyed it". Then Brian escorted him to the door. As Terry stepped onto the street outside he wondered where Ruby was and why did he have to fall in love. As he made his way home his thoughts were of the Boswell's and his love for Ruby and what did the rose tattoo on her neck signified. He knew it was a Gypsy sign, but he wondered as to its significance. He had been walking close to where he'd stumbled over Mr Boswell and wondered about him. Was he around here?. But he didn't see him, or any sign of him. He crossed the street and it was then he heard a child crying. He saw the small girl she was dressed so different than those children he knew. This child was sat on the edge of the streets kerb crying, Her clothes were thin cotton and her hair was tied in a cloth,just like a child he'd once seen in an old video on the screen. A child, yes, he remembered now, it was a child of the city after the war between capitalism and the fascist state leader known as Hitler. From a screen video a period in history many centuries before. He made his way over to the child, who now had stopped crying and then spoke, "what cha want mister?" It was a tongue he'd not heard before but in many ways similar to Mrs Boswell. He asked the child" What's the matter child?.".She looked up at him and he saw that her eyes were wet with tears then she answered him "wats it ta ya Mr?". He asked her "Are you hurt girl?". She answered him "yes I fell over Mister and i lost my balls". He knew that she was referring to the small balls which children played with and sang such ridiculous rhymes in earlier times. It was part of a madness that was known as the playtimes of childhood. He looked down the street then saw the collection of small balls in the gutter hidden from her view. He hurriedly walked to the area and gathered the four balls in his hands and took them to her. She smiled at him took them and put them into her dress pockets and then said "thanks mister I gotta go now, bye". As he watched her as she dissapeared down into a dark hole into the ground on the edge of the street. It was a dark area he'd not noticed before and was intrigued. He followed her, then saw that there were small dirty steps of stone that led down into a much darker domain. He looked around the street and saw that it was completely deserted. It was then that he made another decision based entirely on his intuition and stepped down into the darkness, down below the street.

CHAPTER EIGHT

PASTIMES OF CHILDREN

OLD PLAY STREETS

On the cobbled streets of old town leas
where all the children skipped with dancing feet
where the lamplight shone o'er darkened skies
where the lonesome strangers passed on by

In the streets and shadowed alleyways
where the dogs did bark and children played
where the dust was thick and illness spread
where six children laid all shared one bed

They played amongst their playground dens
where the play some poet laid his pen
where barefoot urchins ran the streets
amongst the demolitions of those dark damp streets
the happiest kids you'd ever meet

Ray Wills

COBBLED STREETS

On the cobbled streets of the old heaths
where the children skipped with dancing feet
where the lamplight shone o'er darkened skies
where the lonesome strangers passed on by
On the streets and shadowed alleyways
where the dogs did bark and children played
where the dust was thick and illness spread
where six children laid and shared one bed

They hid within the playground dens
where the play some poet laid his pen
where barefoot urchins ran the streets
amongst the demolitions of dark damp streets

The children nicked their breakfast rare
amongst the multiracial Fayre
where Pakistani and Caribbean crew
shared their life amongst the brew

The law gave chase and papers spoke
where wise men read of kids elope
where public cry was heard so plain
across the streets of this olé towns lanes

Ray Wills

BACK STREETS

They lived in the back streets
with no boots on their feet but had hearts that were true
the lamplighter lady she lit up each morn
so bright and so early to wake you at dawn
The streets there were narrow and the bread they all shared
there were skipping of ropes and singing of bairn's
the docks they were rich there and the fishes were sweet
with cockles ans winkles and rags on their feet

The rag and bone man rode the streets every week
with horse cart and shouting to all he did greet
there were neighbour's a plenty to help you in need
with cheerful rich chatter and words oh so sweet

The noblemen passed there and rarely did gain
access to the comforts of their little lanes
there were sailors a courting and maids at your door
kisses and promises and soldiers at war

The streets then were cobbled though none did complain
for the richness was theirs down those narrow lanes
with families large and mothers to gain
with another babe wanting in another broods name

The folks they came their from old Waterloo
with stories of gentlemen said how do you do
but the streets they were poor and the children they died
all for the sake of a rich man wealth tide

Ray Wills

ADVENTURE DAYS

They built those big adventure playgrounds
in those pioneering days
we used the best of timber
constructed great walkways
The kids came from the neighbourhood
from two to twenty one
they swung upon those Tarzan swings
oh boy did they have fun

The streets were full of laughter
in those bye gone days
when the kids did all gather there
to while their days away

There were tiny tots and punks with bikes
skin heads and greasers too
little kids in fancy dress and kids with just one shoe

They built their wooden dens there
they painted them real cool
there were tall beams with commando nets
with ramps and slides a few

The games they played were roustabout
run out and give chase
there was laughter on the playgrounds then
with smiles upon each face

We used big tools and hammers
with saws to cut and prime
there were hordes of children playing there
all having special time

The leaders all had long hair
and the kids were satisfied
no health and safety limits then
just common sense and rhymes

Ray Wills

Terry Hewes carefully took the many many steps down deep into the depth of the city. Until he reached the end. Then he found himself in a wide tunnel of concrete with very little lighting. He could hear the echoes of children's voices in the distance. They were singing some old rhyme that he had once discovered on the history screen, They sounded joyful yet very eerie, he caught the words as they echoed through the tunnel. "London bridge is falling down, falling down".

He carried on walking through the tunnel, there was a large area drop within with the metal tracks at its base. Terry followed the sounds of the children's voices. Then he saw the brightly coloured chart on the wall of the tunnel. He went close and saw that it was a diagram of coloured railway lines and places of a mapped network and destinations of the city, some of which he recognised. Then he realised that he was actually in one of the old subways for the one time underground train network. He was surprised that it still existed. As he had been told that such places no longer existed and were a long gone resource of centuries past.

He continued to walk through the subway tunnel following the sounds of the children's voices, The voices got louder now after he had walked some distance. Then he saw the steps to his left which led upwards, he stepped onto the stairway and walked up to the top just a short distance above. Here there was an open doorway to the outside. He realised that he had walked a few miles now. But if his calculations were correct he was still within an area once known as the east end of London south of the city zone. He now could hear the voices distinctly and as he walked out onto the street he saw the terraced rows of houses with iron railing and stone door steps outside each house. Here along the terrace street were children of all ages, both girls and boys. They were all dressed in the styles of a period he guessed as the 20th century. They were all busily involved in those ridiculous time wasting pursuits which were no longer permitted in the modern age. A group of girls were busy, two were holding a long thin rope and twirling it around and over and over and the other girls in the group were busy hopping, skipping and jumping over and through it. As they did so, they were all chanting some ridiculous nonsense rhyme. Meanwhile other girls were throwing small balls against a wall and catching them and also chanting rhymes. As they did so, some lifted their bodies upside down against the walls. As they did so showing off their green knickers and all their underwear which they tucked into their dress. Whilst another group of cheeky boys looked on in somewhat rapture and fits of laughter and pleasure. Other boys were in a large group of rowdy boys of around 8 to 14 years of age. All of these were busy engrossed in kicking, pushing, chasing and kicking out at a rather hard large ball. There seemed to be no logic to this activity, except it was a fact that they had placed their woollen jumpers down at each end some 8 to ten spaces apart. As Terry watched them it seemed to him that this was similar to the soccer which adults played in his neighbourhood. But this was without decent rules of behaviour and conduct. Except a common requirement that no one was to handle the ball. That is no players apart from the boys at each end who stood between the jumpers. It seemed that the whole of the avenue was full of these noisy and mad activities and others. It was a crazy scene and something which he had never seen in his lifetime. Now he knew just why such practices were no longer permitted since the Plague had stopped the gatherings. As Terry walked at a distance and passed by the children he was aware that there was a terrific noise coming from across the road. He followed the direction of the noise as it got louder. He could not see where the noise was coming from, but it looked like it was in a high fenced off piece of land away to the left of the avenue. He hurried along towards the area and then saw the entrance to the site. Its fence was a good ten feet high It was of corrugated tin and above its entrance was a large hoarding. The large sign hoarding was badly painted in gross colours with the words "Mint Street Venture, adults are discouraged from entrance unless escorted by a child". He stopped and pondered should he take a peep inside. The noise within its fence was deafening. There was what sounded like constant hammering and shrieks of children voices shouting and the occasional swear words. Just then he felt a tap on his shoulder and facing him was a youth of probably around 17 years of age. He was dressed in tight blue turned up bottom jeans and an imitation jet black leather jacket with its collars turned up. The youth had long shoulder length hair which hung over his forehead which nearly touched his eyes. The youth spoke "What ya want mush, this errs for kids and you ain't no kid are ya, in fact this whole area is out bounds to your sort". Terry looked at the youth and tried to apologise, but his words didn't come out. The young man spoke again "What kind of geezer are you hanging around kids playgrounds, you needs reporting you do". Terry spoke "I just sort of got lost and wondered what this place is". The youth smiled then said, "OK mush you can take a look this once, im the leader here see and I can escort you". Terry replied, "thank you sir". The youth laughed then said, "Oh its tank you sir is it, what a La de da talker you are no doubt".Then he smiled and said "ok mate come on il show you around, but you cant join in OK?". Terry nodded and followed him in through the large gateway entrance. Then the youth said, "now im gonna educate ya mister". "You see this ere playgrounds on the very land where that Dickens fellah took the idea for his Oliver Twist geezers workhouse". Then he pointed with his right hand and said, "you see over there," he pointed. Then he said,"see those bricks?", "well they be what's left the original workhouse foundations bricks and just down there", again he pointed in another direction and said "You see there was a once an old curiosity shop there". "Which that olé Dickens mush wrote about too, now ya know summit that's not in your fancy learning". As he followed the youth around the muddy area he was amazed at the scene before his eyes. There were literally scores and scores of children of all ages and sizes here. Many were using tools such as saws and hammers and working on building wooden cabins of all shapes and sizes. The noise was very deafening. Other children were madly running around the playground chasing one another. Others were passing pieces of timber to one another and some giving directions on building to other groups. It seemed to be a community of builders with their cabins everywhere all in a state of construction. Then towering above them all was a tall wooden tower made from wooden poles and what looked like ex shuttering boards, all spaced out on walkways. All were extremely high well above ground level, probably twenty feet to forty feet in height. Some of these structures were straddled with thick rope netting. Children were climbing up these structures and swinging on ropes from a great height it looked extremely dangerous and risky. As Terry walked across the site he saw a trail of smoke where a small group was sat around an open fire. They were eating what looked like charcoaled black burnt potatoes. In the far corner of the site was a goat chewing on grass and there were hutches where rabbits no doubt lived. Terry had never before seen anything compared to this place. All the kids looked very dirty but were very happy and absorbed with many laughing and they seemed to be getting great pleasure from these activities. The youth spoke to Terry again, " you v seen the playground mush now bugger off and leave us alone". Terry turned to the young man and said "I am most obliged my friend and thank you for your kindness,im leaving". He stepped outside of the site and crossed the street to where a group of girls were playing a kind of hand clapping routine. They were chanting, "my mother told me she kissed a soldier". And so it went on about a rubber dolly, it was surprisingly full of lots of sexual innuendoes. He walked past the girls and it was then he saw the young girl he'd met on the street earlier. She was busy chanting a similar rhyme to another girl. " Down in the brambles down down by the sea, true love to you my darling true love to me and when were married we l raise a family true love to you darling, true love to me." Then the girl saw him and she ran to greet him and took his hand and smiled at him and she said, "oh thank you mister for finding my balls". Then she asked him "Are you staying here?", "cause you know its not allowed!,"she said. He replied," no im not staying here" then he said, "I know im not allowed, I just visited your venture place". She smiled at him and said "i hope to see you again Mister". Then she smiled at him again then she ran off back to join her companion. Terry walked back down the avenue leading to the steps which led down to the subway underground system. Just then his wrist watch bleeped "dam it," he said and reached it and slid the micro phone out, putting it in his ear and spoke "yes". It was a woman's voice,he recognised it,it was Ruby. "Where are you Terry?. I miss you,"she said. He was shocked that she had access to his phone. But replied, "sorry Ruby, I have been busy been visiting a friend and now im on my way back home". She asked him "Why have you not been back here?" she asked "its complicated" he replied "its something to do with my position at work". She spoke, "you could have said so Terry". "Can we meet up soon?" she asked "I need to talk Terry". He answered her " Look ive got your number registered here now

Ruby, i will ring you back tomorrow and arrange something". She spoke "OK Terry, I love you". Then the phone bleeped and went dead then he slid it back into his watch. Then he walked down the steps into the subway and began the long walk back. Then later when he reached the familiar outskirts of his home zone it was dark and he was tired. He made his way to his apartment and used his password at the entrance and he was so glad that he was home. All that night Terry was troubled. He was wondering just how Ruby had obtained access to his phone. For only the higher ranking members of the organisation could gain this apart from those close to him who he gave it to. As he laid in bed that night he thought of her Ruby and how much he missed her. But at the same time was wondering what she wanted and would it be safe to ses her would it jeopardise his standing in the organisation. His head was full of questions. He thought of his recent adventures with the children in the underground, which was prohibited territory and he could be in real trouble. He wondered how were they able to survive in their world. Why was the organisation unaware of their existence, or more fascinating was the thought they they may not be totally unaware. His head was full of questions. Where were their parents? did they have any?. His thoughts were in confusion they were all jumbled up and his experiences were contrary to what he had learned as a pioneer of the organisation. These young people were dirty and crazy they were all involved in very risky pursuits and yet they were very happy and contented. Then he fell into a deep sleep and dreamt of being with her and of her love for him.

CHAPTER NINE

THE WAKE UP CALL

SEEKERS OF THRUTH

In the schools of man's philosophies
the annuals tell the tale
the conflicts of aspirations
just like the dreamers at the well

The poets and the writers
the men of virtues fame
are written there in parchment
though in another's name

The stories of the wars they fought
the quarrels and the truce
the words of wisdom spoken
from the sages young in Truth

The consequence of battles
were blowing n the sand
like pictures of illusions
though they played the victors hand

The sacred robes of Honour
they wore a noble crest
with one eye on the victor
they danced a pirouette

The landscapes of forgiveness
all the sad bitter regrets
were painted out in words of verse
where Truth awaits one yet

The forests of the unicorns
the mythical refrains
where ladders of the sacred names
are freedom and regret
under another's name

Though verse and rhyme held no one accord
their phrases were divine
they humbled their transgressions
then sent them down the line

From Socrates and Plato times
to Dylan of today
they preached of Truth and freedom
whilst bullets went astray

Oh words of understanding
were written from the cross
whilst man burnt all his bridges
the Truth of life was lost.

Ray Wills

STORY TELLERS

He listened to their stories
each night around the yog
long times ago now
but still vivid in their minds
The crack of the whip
the tears and the shame
the plantation voyages
from the old donkey lanes

The old Gypsy Queen
and the King of the rings
the stories they told
whilst the pretty gal's sings

The miner birds singing
and the catapult sling
like the rabbits we chased
on the first days of spring

The fairgrounds
were busy then
with plenty to see
the barters of horses
and the walks on the leas

The heathers and flowers
they sold in the square
pretty gold bands
to wrap around their hair

The travellers laments
and the Caroline songs
the paintings of Picasso
and the art work of Augustus John

The vardos and wheelwrights
the Smiths and tins
where soldiers of fortune
told their tales on a whim
The nights around the yog
where the stew pot did boil
in Grandfathers times
when we were just boys
with the Warrens and Turners
Coopers and Kings

When Stanley's sold ponies
and Lees lived so free
in the forests and high lanes
which led to the sea

The folki that sailed ships
to Newfoundland too
across oceans and rivers
to seek liberty from Poole

On the new England campsite
and their little Egypt home
once upon a dream now
where visions once roamed

Ray Wills

STEVENSONS DAYS

Next to the bathroom
at the top of the stairs
i remember as children
we all said our prayers

The lines of the tables
and verse oh so neat
the manners of gentlefolk
we all learned to speak

There was food on the table
though the morsels were meek
we were strong in our culture
and our language was weak

We learnt from our masters
and held back our tears
as we curtsied and frolicked
throughout our play years

The poets were sound then
with lines oh so sweet
there were hawkers and pedlar's
all run down the streets
The air it was cold
and the hares they did run
the farmland was plentiful
by the roar of the gun

The fables and stories
we were all told
our heroes were wise men
and the hills made of gold

The church bells they rang
and the congregation grew
there was laughter abroad then
and boats sailed from Poole

RAY WILLS

CANDLE LIGHT DREAMERS

Candlelight dreamers born in the dark
childhood with playmates and rides in the park
skies full of starlight and moonbeams on show
carousel maidens in Gods rodeo

Whispers and wishes promises free
kisses and blushes hugs all for thee
paradise angels with dust on their wings
fairies and goblins and old sparkly tins

Lovers and sweethearts down by the sea
night winds a blowing in old histories
hands held and whispers and guns fired at dawn
sand, sea and fishes and old stories worn

Crystals and jewellery that sparkles so fine
long lost book pages like old father times
rocking horse memories and days by the sea
cock-ells and muscles and old histories

Touched by her poetry with words lost online
like heartstrings of ecstasy lost to the blind
farewells and greetings rolled into one
kisses and forethought all bundled in fun

Annals and book fairs with words flying free
like sandals of hippies and old revelries
sown by the poets in heavy blue tones
crafted and reasoned and sweet were her moans

Down by the meadows over the streams
where willow trees hung
and beauty it screamed

art form in reason was lost in the tide
where the bird song was music
to the groom and the bride

Ray Wills

HEAVENLY THOUGHTS

I used to think that heaven
was just a thought away
where the sun it shone there daily
and the children they all played
Where lambs did chase the hillsides
and the sparrows sang its tune
where daisies spread their garlands
all in the month of June

I used to cherish moments
when friends all came to call
where words were spoken softly
and kings were brave and tall

Where love was sweet and innocent
and romance was true to dream
where rivers flowed across the lands
and farm lands set the scenes

Where hedge grows were so rich in fruit
and vardos rolled the downs
where songbirds filled the sky each day
and the victor wore a crown
Where poets wrote of Camelot
and carousels did spin
where maids were dancing in the yard
and life was free of sin

The castles on the hillsides
with moats and drawbridge grand
where goldfiches nestled in the boughs
and sweethearts all held hands

Ray Wills

He woke up later than usual to the wonderful sounds of the goldfinch birds singing outside of his windows and the sunshine's rays. He thought how lucky he was to hear their song each day. They seemed to sing no matter the weather. He got showered then got dressed. He had thought over his situation and decided to leave the phone call to Ruby until later. He spent most of the morning on the screen looking up the childhood history. Particularly the children's street games rhymes and adventure playground. He needed answers to the questions of why these pastimes were no longer in existence in the present order and yet remained underground. Why did these children in the underground exist and what was the secret of their great pleasure from such idle activities?. The computer screen came up with a lot of history of the period from the 1920s to the plagues. There was an organisation set up in the late 1920s with royal consent to safeguard recreational activities. Namely the national playing fields association. Then during the war years of 1939-1945 many children were playing amongst the bombed out cities of Europe. They were playing with debris and junk material from the bombed houses. Many creating their own communities play houses and dens from iron, wood. bricks and stone. In Germany such a place was Emdrupt junk playground. After the war a Lady Marjorie Allen from the English Nurseries Association visited there and returned to the UK with radical idea. She saw how these children were happily employed in these junk playgrounds and campaigned to set up such playgrounds run by trained play leaders in the heart of the cities. Her cause was supported by the National Playing Fields Association and they set up trial playgrounds in the cities. These proved successful and as a result numerous community associations and councils operated these junk playgrounds. Though the name was changed from junk to adventure to make them more acceptable to the country at large. Over many decades the NPFA funded these initiatives and they were co opinionated trough their offices at Playfield house London, By the 1970s there were hundreds of these playgrounds operating throughout Europe. Films were made and campaigns were instrumental such as the Fair play for children and Children Waiting film. Regional play associations were established by the NPFA to encourage the growth of play facilities. Then the

European governments enforced the health and safety acts which took the risk factor out of child's play and there were many cutbacks in services all around and at the same time. These factors were instrumental in removing many of these playgrounds to a small limited number of original sites. Then the NPFA s own funding was cut along with the Fair Play for Children and others and many of the employees and organisations were lost. Many children no longer had access to such play facilities. Then in time the NPFA executive made changes to their own function they returned to saving recreational playing fields only. Along with a name change. They became known as Fields In Trust. No longer was the word playing in their title. Following the plague years such play spaces were totally removed and replaced with areas where play was limited. Many of these areas had large prohibitive notices displayed in prominent positions on site stating "no running, jumping, noise or risk taking activities". Whilst the children's rhymes on streets and playgrounds which "the Opies" catalogued were made to be not politically correct and other measures introduced to limit their use via the various safety acts. Games with conkers was made an offence. Children's play was eventually removed also as a result of the use of micro phones and screens for educational purposes and open air activities were discouraged as being unsafe. He knew that Childhood no longer was a designated life period. The years leading up to Adulthood were fortunately now spent in educational constructive pursuits and preparation for future pioneering possibilities. He read the text and studied the artists impressions amongst the high resolution of original photos of the pre war, war and post war period. The photos of children on the streets similar to which he'd actually witnessed first hand himself recently in the underground. Here were also photos most back and white also of children in the process of building their wooden dens in the adventure playgrounds. All very similitude to the one in the olde world community at Southwark s Mint street adventure playground. He wondered what Dickens himself would think of these events if he were alive today wondered if he would approve of the changes made to improve society and to make it all so much easier to live full lives. As he studied the screens images he wondered if in fact the modern life had lost something in seeking perfection. Taking away the risk maybe limited man's growth and development. He wondered if in fact we would have developed much stronger as people if we had allowed natural growth to take place despite all its setbacks of wars and disease. He would never know. He wondered if love was an explicate necessity and if sexual pleasure from man and woman to create life was what it was all about. Many thoughts crossed his mind,including the man woman relationship. Was it destined to develop or was it eventually to be set aside for the natural sexual desires of each to be paramount rather than the partnerships family situations. These were questions he did not know the answer for. Although he now knew that being in love was emotionally painful as well as pleasurable.

As he scanned the range of studies on the subject of child hood he was aware that messages were coming through. He saved the information and photos then pressed the green button and the screen changed. The new screen lit up with two new headings, He chose the most recent one. It was a message from Brian. It read "Hi Terry, just to let you know I can see you again next Monday at my place.". "I've had a good look at your micro doc and like it". "We need to talk Terry, I have some news for you but it will wait till next week". "Hope you found your way back home OK, without falling over anyone". "See you next week usual place and time". Then he was gone. Terry wondered why Brian had mentioned him falling over someone. He thought about it and it bothered him. Also the fact that he had not told Brian about his meeting with the Boswell's. He wondered if Brian knew a lot more than he was saying and how did he know. Then he clicked onto the next message on the screen below and the screen in front of him automatically changed. The new screen lit up before him. He recognised it for it had the organisations familiar eagle and birds emblem heading in gold. He knew this was what what he was waiting for. The screen suddenly changed and a figure of an official of the organisation was before him live on the screen. The official spoke. "Good day Terry Hewes, the committee have studied your report in some depth." ." We apologise for the delay in getting back to you". "However we had to check back with our department your safety checks and discovered some discrepancies".The official continued "We have now passed your personal details on to the head of our security department for further study they will contact you at sometime soon". He continued "However,your reports findings and recommendation were however approved with some changes, based on your background within the organisation". "Our superior security officer Ms Cordell will be in touch with you shortly". Then the screen bleeped and he was gone. The screen reverted back to his former study on childhood. Terry was left very confused. He wondered what the problem was that they needed to check him out again,Hadn't he had a thorough security check a while ago after his pioneering had ended. Then he realised the name that they threw at him. It was Cordell. It troubled him greatly. It was the name Ruby had been using. Surely it wasn't Ruby?,surely she wasn't its top security officer?. Then he thought there must be many in the organisation with that name, Surely it must be a coincidence, but the thought troubled him greatly. Then he remembered that he had promised to phone Ruby back today to make an arrangement to see her. He decided to close the screen down for today and phone her. He switched the screen off then he slipped the micro phone out of his wrist watch and rang Ruby's number. There was silence then a buzz that told him she wasn't connected. He would try again later. He decided to go out for a walk he needed the exercise. Terry made his way out into his forecourt past the honeysuckle and the sounds of the goldfinch song and began the walk. He looked up and saw that the traffic was busy overhead today with many of the vehicles pilot less, yet full. As he walked his familiar city home zone he felt uneasy. He knew he was being watched as everyone was. As his movements were up there on the big screen. But this feeling was different, he felt uneasy and knew that things were not right. Ruby wasn't connected, Brian was keeping something from him and the organisation were checking up on him. It didn't look good. He crossed the city line and made his way towards the mansions. Shortly after he found himself in the area where he had seen the young girl child the day before. But today there was no one there. He saw the pavement where he had followed the girl down the stone steps. He crossed over the street to the very spot and was surprised to see that there was now a large metal cover over the hole. He looked around, the street was deserted and even the sky above was now empty of traffic. He took the edge of the cover in his hands and with some physical effort he heaved and lifted it. Then he somehow managed to slide the cover aside. Revealing the dark hole and the stone steps. He stealth fully made his way down the steps into the depth of the hole and as he did so he heard laughter of children far below. The he made his way down the steep stone steps being careful not to slip. Eventually he was at the bottom at its base and the entrance to the subway. The noise of children laughter and cries were louder now. He hurriedly made his way along the dark underground subway but in the opposite direction from previously. He wanted to explore and the noise was coming from that direction this time and was different he heard dogs barking and water running. He hurriedly made his way along the old underground subway reading the names of the stations on the walls as he did so. His route was towards the Tower, he knew from history that he was close to the Thames and the area known as Kenning-ton. Then he saw some stone steps on the side of the tunnel leading upwards. He stepped onto the bottom step and then he read the sign on the wall. It read GALLERY in bright large red lettering. He then climbed the steep steps and then found himself at the entrance to an old red brick building. Its brickwork was dark red and with its dark brown wooden heavy beams structure it looked very old. He pushed the green doors entrance doors inwards and he entered the building. He found himself inside its main room. Which was very long, its ceiling was very high and it was decorated throughout with emblems and designs of heraldry, in coats of paint of green and red. Along its walls were what looked like rows upon rows of white coated cards. As he moved along these rows he disturbed the thick layers of the white dust and these flew into the air around him and made him cough. His cough echoed. As the white dust lifted, it floated and moved. He saw that it was deep and it covered row upon row of what looked like cards. He crossed to the row close by and touched the thick white dust and it lifted into the air. He saw that the white dust covered the thick coloured cards, which he now saw close up had written inscriptions. He moved his hand upon one of these and felt its firmness and depth. He lifted it with his hand and saw that it wasn't just a card but was a cover and within its bindings full of thin sheets of white paper within its thick card cover. He flicked the pages of papers in his hand and saw that each one had texts and also pictures. He held it firmly in his hands and felt its depth and texture. On its cover in large script were the words A TALE OF TWO CITIES the authors name was faded. Then he realised that he had discovered items which were once known as books. Such articles were written published in large quantities and read by countless multitudes of people in the past centuries. These were now relics and regarded as worthless items. The white thick dust which covered these were a consequence of age. Many of the pages within these books were no doubt dust too. This was obviously one of the major sources of cultural necessity of the age. Known as libraries. These were now prohibited and out of bounds to members of the new world order. Such places were said to encourage anti government activity and dangerous material. There were known writers, authors who made a fortune from the sales of such books. He had been instructed to the dangers of these people and their books whilst undertaking his pioneer training. Names such as Orwell,Huxley, Wells and Marx were all banned from the modern world. For they and others were believed to have encouraged rebellion and terrorism. He coughed again for the airways here was full of the white dust. He made his way back out of the building and into the clearer air. When he got his thoughts together he made his way back into the underground subway. As he was about to walk back the way he'd come his phone bleeped. It was Ruby. She spoke softly "Terry I cant speak for long my phone was cut off and im using another,can we meet up today whilst im free?". Terry answered " Hi love, yes, but il be a while depends where you want to meet". She said "well are you still in the city zone?". He answered "well my apartments there, do you want to come there Ruby?" she answered,"Yes if that's OK","ive got to be careful though Terry". She said "its best if I come later, when its dark Terry". He said "Yes that's good Ruby,say about 20,00 hours". Then he started to give her his address but before he could finish the sentence her phone line went dead and she was cut off. He slipped the micro phone back into his watch and hurried on his way back. The time on his watch read 1600 hours. He needed to get back quickly to shower and eat. Hopefully Ruby would be able to phone back at some time. He wondered what was happening to her she sounded very wary and scared. He hurriedly made his way back to his apartment. It was getting cooler now that the sun was going down. But as he approached his home zone then his apartment building he saw the goldfinch swarming on the sky above him. Their song was so beautiful today. It was so good to be home. When he got in he went to the screen and ordered a set of silver ear rings a last present for Ruby.

CHAPTER TEN

TRUST

NIGHT GIRL

The bottle of perfume lay opened
though all her dreams were left on the shelf
along with her virtue and innocence
all abandoned like nobody else

The room she had let from the sandman
that's when he happened to call
with her daydreams all carefully packed there
her dreams left out in the hall

The windows were shuttered and drawn there
with her eyes all lifted in prayers
like the kisses shed shed in the moonlight
with lovers who'd knocked on her door

The candle was lit in the night air
the wax was settled and free
though the flame it was lit in the darkness
upon the hour of three

Her suitors had left in the moonlight
along with her faded refrains
from a song that she stole from a beggar
they called her calamity Jane

The lipstick red and so smeary
the dress she wore was so rare
along with her shoes and her attire
her hair and her innocence bared

The night it told all her stories
her tales of woe lost to none
though her wishes were cast in the moonlight
her heart was set just for one

The cat in the alley meowed there
the tramp in the gutter slept on
with the drunks and the pathways to Venus
the stories went rolling along

The clock in the hall set at midday
the bridal gown hung in the room
along with the pictures he'd left there
with faded love letters he'd crooned

The sleep that she took was disturbed there
the night air spoke her refrains
along with the shadows of past tense
the magic was gone once again

Ray Wills

WISDOM TALES

They shared their wisdom around the campfires
with the stories that they told
some were wise and thoughtful others wise and old

The grandfathers of time
whispered their stories of the past
but the hands of time were ticking
and they knew it wouldn't last

Oh the travellers and the nomads
like the merry tales of gain
when the yog was hot and fiery
and the wind was in your veins

When the spirit in you lifted
and your soul was sure to soar
with one eye on the wise one
and the other born to score

Oh the trails were long and winding
where the tracks were set in sand
like the cartwheels that kept turning
and the dreams of every man

How the elders loved the country
with its nature and its plains
when men were free to listen
and the coyotes howled again

Those days they will remember
like the tales that wise men spoke
till the modern ways were on us and the media it woke

Whilst the kids were still in wonder
and the rabbits all ran free
before their ways were sanctioned

in the pages of our history's

The fingers pressed the buttons
and the pictures were in store
with news flashing there daily
and the children lost at wars

Whilst the old uns
still had memories
whilst wise man walked alone

The micro chip society was set to fashions free
on the highways of the broadband
all were blinded by the free
in a world of spin and freedom
they lost their liberties

Ray Wills

IN THE DARKEST OF HOURS

When your heart lies empty
but your love is full
spare a thought for me darling
and il spare a thought for you

In the darkest night times
when the day is through
spare a thought for me darling
il spare a thought for you

When the romance is over
when the dust has settled too
spare a thought for me darling
and il spare a thought for you

When my glass is half empty
when your glass is half full
in the darkest of hours
il be thinking of you

Ray Wills

Ruby Boswell was scared as she made her way through the city streets. She wore a headscarf a long dress and a heavy raincoat to attempt to hide her appearance. It was dark though there was a full moon and starlit night sky. She went into areas of the main routes the side zones it was a long ways around. But it was best considering all things. She knew they were on to her. She saw their secret society rooms. Where functions were held and only the very best of top ranking members attended. Here they were treated to shows of the very best young woman in scanty underwear and less. Every night members were entertained there by they scanty clad girls and later in private rooms they were entertained by more intimate ladies. She had been there off and on for over three years now and during that time she had access to many members private lives. She had become accepted and given special privileges. Someone was asking her lots of personal asked questions. Then just recently this had all changed someone had followed her when she left in the evening. Somehow they knew rumour got out that she was working for an underground group of gypsies and others whose aims were to gradually change the organisation aims and objectives. As a result she was now on the run. She knew that Terry could be trusted and she had made the decision tonight she would totally confide in him. She had made copies of the most secretive documents she discovered and had access to all the addresses of members including Terry's address. She knew that Terry was her only avenue.

Brian Deleaux was relaxing in the members suite on the third floor of the centre. He had just attended a members committee meeting . They had discussed Terry's position in the ranking and his role. For the past few years he had specifically been following the education progress of the latest bright boy Terry Hewes. He had built up a trusting relationship with him and was able to monitor his progress totally unbeknown to Terry. But just recently there had been a problem. He had followed Terry movements after one of his regular visit to Brian's apartment. He discovered that Terry had broken the rules of the group. He was not only going into prohibited territory's and mixing with underground groups of Gypsies and wayward children. But that he was having sexual relationships with one of the Gypsies. A girl who had managed to give a false name and had somehow managed to get herself in a position in this very premises. Fortunately the group were able to remove her from her position, The organisation were at present processing Terry's own position particularly as he was one if the groups greatest success. Going through the pioneering and now writing micro reports for future educational programs. Yes Terry Hewes had become somewhat of a threat. They had however recently given him false information on the Gypsy girl that she was prominent in the organisations structure. As Brian sat there in the club room he was thinking of how Terry had trusted him and how he had through Terry discovered that network of conspirators via the Gypsy girl and now the group were about to access their phones and services to halt their growth in the future. Brain knew the Ruby girl and had both admired her and desired her. He watched her working in the centre and on one occasion had approached her for sexual favours. But she declined. Which was a pity though he knew that he could use his influence to work on her in the future in more ways than one.

Terry Hewes was waiting. He had not heard back from Ruby and it was getting dark. He had showered, eaten and had changed his clothes to something more comfortable. A light rayon shirt and a pair of fashionable blue cotton jeans. He wanted to look his best if and when Ruby arrived. His watch read just 1908 hours. There was still time for a phone call and her visit wasn't till 2000 hours. He checked his screen for messages, but there were none apart from a constant bleep. He wondered why he was getting interference, maybe he would have it checked soon it could have been hacked. He sat in his arm chair and his head was full of inconsistencies and questions he needed to resolve. Perhaps Ruby knew something, though he was concerned that she could be involved in the higher ranks of the organisation. He wished he'd talked it all through with Brian . He should have confided with Brian, especially about his visits to the Boswell and the child's playgrounds. He above anyone would be able to advise him and help him understand his concerns. He wondered why the underground Gypsy communities in the east of the city were able to operate without the organisation members being aware. Then there were all those children throughout the underground subway system. Its like they were living in a time zone there all trapped there in a period of history long past. He thought how happy they were though in their risky playtimes pursuits and it bothered him. Then he relaxed as he laid back in his chair and fell asleep. He woke up suddenly by the sounds of his musical jingly doorbell, it was playing a rendition of the 18th 12th overture. He went over to his screen and pressed the green button on the screen and D for door. The picture came up on the screen he recognised her it was Ruby, but she looked overdressed. He pressed OK and as he did so he heard the door slide open and his recorded voice said "Welcome come in". He pressed the off button and the screen went off but the buzz noise remained in the background. He walked across the room and made his way to meet her. He was surprised by her appearance she looked overdressed in a long ankle length rain coat and with an ugly red and brown scarf covering most of her face. She smiled then she was in his arms and he held her tight Then he saw her tears then tasted her lips he held her hand and led her to his lounge She said "wait Terry ive got to get my coat off" she removed her scarf and smiled at him. Then she spoke," I don't think anyone saw me, but if they did its doubtful they would know me" she said. He laughed as he helped her remove her heavy raincoat. He threw it aside then he hurriedly led her to his bedroom.

It was early morning when Ruby Boswell woke. Terry was still sleeping soundly next to her. She was glad that she was with him here she felt safe. She was so glad that she had told him everything including all about her past life. All the men she had known all those who said they loved her, yet hurt her. Told him of her past alcohol addiction and her work at the centre. Of the men and women there who made the rules. Rules which they themselves did not follow. She told him of her past relationship with Bert at the yard who made love to her like she had never known, but wouldn't leave his wife and kids for her. She told Terry all about the group she belonged to. The folks who banded together to work towards defeating the organisation and its structure. Amongst them were Gypsies and the underground people. She confided to Terry all about her abortion, the child she never brought up. Bert's child. Terry had told her about his involvement within the organisation and his friendship with Brian and his experience in the underground world. He was concerned that the organisation was watching him now for his screen computer was being hacked and he was concerned for Ruby's safety. He had given her the late birthday present hed bought. She loved the set of ear rings. Ruby watched him as he lay there next to her so vulnerable like a child but so intelligent. She knew that he came from a long Gypsy line of great people. She thought how he had made love to her cherishing her through the night and she cuddled into his naked body and felt him stir and sigh. As she lay there she heard the familiar sounds of the dawn chorus she recognised it as the song of the goldfinch. Living by the heath close to the lane she had been brought up to their familiar song and the family had bred the canary with the finch to produce the lovely musical tone of the miner birds. When Terry had chatted with her he'd told her of all the goldfinch birds outside the Mansions where Brian lived and had mentioned the birds here too. With their delightful singing. Having been involved in the trapping of goldfinch in the thistles as a young girl she knew all there was to know about breeding these songbirds. These were the Gypsy travellers friends. She wandered over to the window and watched them darting in and out of the forecourt singing their familiar tune. She noticed these birds were all of the same size larger than the ones she saw on the heath. But were still very familiar with their unique coats and beautiful songs. Just then as if by magic they all were gone and there was no sign of them in the hedgerows flowers or in the clear blue early morning sky. Then she felt the arms around her the cloth over her mouth. She couldn't breath and then she felt needle in her arm and she slept. They took her silently in the early hours whist Terry was sleeping.

CHAPTER ELEVEN

REVOLVING DOORS

REVOLVING DOORS

He stepped inside the revolving door
hear the echoing footsteps down the halls
the corridors drab and mean
cries of despair lives that might have been

The pin down pressures the shots in the dark
psychiatric moments up with the lark
the screams of hollow words expressed
anguish and moments left with the rest

The doctors minutes hurry bye
bipolar moments how time flies
acute psychotic dreams no less
a world lay shattered speech unheard
the staff drew lots and smoked their fags
another time another drag

Ray Wills

MELANCHOLY MOMENT

In a melancholy moment I took a look at my life
my cupboards laid empty with troubles and strife
the world sure looked crazy close up and more
laid back i viewed it those darker moments and all

Then from a distance i saw the sun rise
heard all their whispers and lies then gazed into her eyes
her smile was infectious it turned the tide
the volume was drowning but her love was denied
full of surprise

In a melancholy moment i surveyed it all
the world was in crisis as never before
her smile was enticing it led me astray
into my arms she fell forever a day

My dreams were rich and full of fun
she was my girl my number one
the moment was past my life had begun

Ray Wills

THE CHECK OUT

I checked out the Truth in shadows
as a way to set one free
free from understanding
the world to you and me

I travelled through the highways
where priests and poets hide
way out in the outback
in stories tall and wide

The cat sat at the table
where the dogs ate all their scraps
no word was uttered in the night
no misfits read the map

The flags were waving freely
though the lies were set in stone
the people took it all as fact
then headed off for home

The common touch was awesome
he told it to the crowds
too many yet to number
to few to talk out loud

The cards were on the table
spread out for all to see
with the joker and the blank one
hiding truth and honesty

Where wise men took their counsel
where ignorance was blessed
where Donald turned his trump card
where Hitlers name was jest

They turned the wheels in motion
then handed me their claim
whilst refuge was denied to souls
they cursed the prophets name

Ray Wills

B rian Deleaux sat amongst the committee members. Everyone was busy chatting and sharing information. All waiting for the chair its president to start the meeting. Today's meeting was called as an extraordinary meeting the result of a situation occurring within its ranks which could jeopardise its progress. Brian had received regular reports from his flights androids birds daily over the past weeks. Reports which he had brought along to the attention of this special meeting. A meeting arranged to discuss the situation and decide what to do. These were unusual circumstances where a former high raking pioneer had crossed the line of prohibition. Just then a hush fell in the conference room as he rose waved and all sat down, The President made his way to the prominent chair and spoke "Good morning consulate". There was a good morning echo from those present and music played a bird song melody. Then their president spoke "Has everyone received the copies of the agenda?" he asked. All nodded "Then I will begin with my talk" he said. "Good morning all persons present, as most of you know ive had the position of musical director for many years and now im retired from that former formal position and been able to concentrate on my hobbies". "However I have come out of retirement on this occasion. This is a matter of some grave importance urgency and could effect our organisations standing worldwide" he said. He continued addressing the committee "Up till now our organisation has been in a prominent position worldwide in the new world order". "As you know my own success has been in flight androids of artificial birds,I have developed a worldwide successful project to its fulfilment"." That of creating flights of android drone birds which resemble goldfinch in appearance and in song". He continued "These birds have been able to mix within the wilds alongside the common birds of the heaths and have observed the lives of the vagrant workforce in the prohibited zones. Those who are employed in creating the necessary brickworks pottery and coal". "As you know these areas are out of bounds to our people prohibited and there are strict penalties imposed on those who disobey". "These vagrants gypsies have until now been quite happy in their diseased polluted environments and their children in their underground worlds of foolishness" He continued "We have been quite pleased to leave them there under our control."". "However we now have unfortunately a situation as one of our most intelligent members has created a problem.". "He who actually has been successfully involved in helping us to further our aims and objectives has himself got embroiled in both contacts within the gypsy vagrants world, as well as seduction of one of its members". "These activities have alarmed me because the person is in face one of my most intelligent students". "I have received micro film of him in compromising situations with a young gypsy woman." "Gained from micro film through my Android drone goldfinches". "The person in question has also been in discussions with members of an underground movement to destroy our great advances". "The girl his partner we discover was actually involved in our social centre and has dangerous inside information only permitted to our prestige members". "This is a serious situation, for not only is the person in question an aspiring member of our body but is in fact from a gypsy traveller ancestry". "We need to make a decision on this matter as soon as possible both him and the girl are being watched and their micro phone and their screens are being monitored daily". "Our select committee are at present reading his reports which are excellent, which give the impression that he is fully behind our plans for the future as his ideals are profound". "Therefore we need to make a decision today on actions immediately to resolve this before our people become aware of the underground workers and their world". "We have made great progress to date this could jeopardise our future position worldwide within the new order". "Today I ask you all to Please make your ideas known".

Terry woke from his sleep he was alone. He called out her name "Ruby" "Where are you?". But there was no answer. Though he could hear the sounds of the goldfinches song outside. He looked at his wrist watch it read 8000 hours. He had slept a long time. Much more than usual it wasn't normal for him to oversleep. Then he remembered his dreams and his sleep which was disturbed by the sounds of a great many birds in flight and their song. He took his micro phone out from his watch and rang her number, but it was dead.

Ruby Boswell awoke it was dark in fact it was pitch black she reached out for Terry in the darkness but he wasn't there. The bed was hard for some reason and she was cold. She turned in the darkness and realised she was in another bed and in another room. She looked around and as her eyes got accustomed to the darkness she saw other beds. She realised she was in a large dormitory. She had heard of such places from her family. She heard someone snore and another turn in her sleep. She looked for her clothes but couldn't see them anywhere. She looked down and realised she was wearing a thin white cotton night dress and was completely naked beneath it. Then she heard a women's voice come from the bed next to her. "Your new here aren't you dear" she said. Ruby could just make out the women's face in the darkness she was young too, but had an old face as though in pain. The woman spoke again," I heard them bring you in earlier, you were crying and they gave you a shot" she said. Ruby felt cold and weak. "Where am I?" she asked. The woman replied "This is a rest place, they put you in here to help you cope with life if youv had a hard time". Ruby looked at her and asked "Who,who are they?" she asked. The woman replied "Well the doctors of course", She said "They help a lot a lot of disturbed people and lots folks with fancy ideas." "Those with lots of conspiracy theorists and folks believe there's a God and talk to him and other bad stuff". "This place is a bit of a revolving door we seem to get a lot in here who keep coming back" she said"Why, theyl soon get you well and sorted out though" she said. "What's your name?" she asked "Oh its Ruby" she replied "my names Ruby Boswell". The woman smiled and said, "Oh my names Ruth Durrant, but I would keep quiet bout your surname in here if I were you Ruby love as some these folk don't like gypping people". "Also some these gal's in here are queer buggers too"she said. "so you will need to be on your guard"."Its all part their sickness, so be careful Ruby"." A lot of them in here have Bipolar and some got what the Doctor calls acute psychotic disorders and can be very nasty". Ruby said "Thanks Ruth". Ruby looked around and saw the long corridor of beds and then pulled the blanket over herself and cried herself to sleep.

Ruby slept well and was woken by aloud alarm going off and hearing people shouting and running down the corridors. Then all went quiet. She looked around the room it was now light and now she could see all the beds and they were empty. The woman called

Ruth was gone. Then she heard a man's voice "Good afternoon" he said. He was a tall man distinguished looking she guessed he was a doctor. He looked the part, mature and confident. He spoke, "my name is Johnstone". "im your doctor" he said. "Youv had a long sleep Ruby". "Are you hungry"? he asked." Yes" she said "of course im dam hungry and why am I in here"? she asked. He answered her, "Your not a a well person" he said. "We had to constrain you"." You had some bad thoughts"he said. He smiled then said"we are here to help you get back to the good life". He smiled at her again and then said "Il take you down to the kitchen if you like ,you can eat a hearty breakfast from the computer there". "Where's my clothes "?she asked. He replied "We had to destroy them" he said. Then he said. "there's some clothes your size on the side there" he pointed to the table nearby. "Everything's there is your size" he said. Then once again he said,"Once your dressed come down to eat and then later we will have a nice talk". "I don't want to talk"she said"I just want to go home." He spoke again " you will go home, once your back to good health". Then he said"Il be back later".Then he walked away. Ruby swore under her breath.

Then she walked over to the table and began looking through the clothes that were there but they were all dark,formal and dreary looking. Not at all like the pretty dresses she was used to wearing. But she found a few items she could wear and she dressed hurriedly. Then she heard the doctor he had returned. "Oh good" he said "I See youv found some suitable clothes Ruby and are dressed". He smiled at her and commenced to ask her a series of questions about her thoughts. She was beginning to get annoyed and swore. He smiled at her again and said "You are displaying irrational emotions and we can help you through this". She said "I'm not stupid I know your game I heard about these places". The doctor said "I don't know what youv heard but this is a centre to help folks like you with their bad thoughts and help you through your condition you can go for lunch now and I will let you settle in and start you on your programme tomorrow". "I will show you to the social room now and you can come with me and meet everyone".Ruby apprehensively followed him out of his office then down the long corridor.

Terry wondered why Ruby had left without telling him. He went over in his mind was it something he had said that evening which made her decide to leave. But he count think of a valid reason she seemed so happy with him. He decided to look for her, but first he would contact Brian and seek his assistance. If anyone would know what to do it was Brian. He realised he would have to be honest and up front with him and hoped that he would understand and help. He went to the screen and pressed the button. The screen lit up but then it want off, "Dam it" he said "that's all I need". He pressed again but it was dead. "Well il just have to turn up at the Mansions and hope he's in" he said. He dressed into his shirt top and jeans then he made his way out into the courtyard. He was surprised that the birds were not there singing their lovely medley for as it was a lovely day. Then he started his walk to Brian's apartment.

It was a good hour before he arrived there. It was then he saw all of the goldfinch birds were gathered there on the stone floor of Brian's forecourt they all seemed to be very still as if they were stoned. He walked towards them but they never moved. He thought this was very strange. When he got close to them he knew why. They were all android drones exquisitely designed as goldfinches. These were all of the same size and mechanical and yet now were stone dead. He stood there for a while just looking at them his mind was racing. He wondered why were these here outside of Brian's apartment block. Surely they cant be the same birds he's seen regularly here on his visits singing such lovely melodies. He looked again at their designs, it was extremely difficult to see the differences from the real natural birds. They all had superb imitation plumage feathers and the familiar gold makings. His mind was questioning, what if all the goldfinches were he saw daily were all drones. If so they would have recorded his movements from here to the Boswell's home. Then the terrible thought came into his head what if Brian knew. What if the birds at his own place those outside his own apartment. Those which sang outside around his own honeysuckle plants were also mechanical drone songbirds. In which case they would in no doubt know his every movement. Then thought came into his head that if so they could they be recording everything particularly if they have minute cameras in their design. The thought troubled him greatly and he wondered if

Brian was in some way involved and could be responsible for all these drones their designs and their songs. The thought entered his mind that Brian could actually be instrumental in the whole thing. He looked up towards Brian's window which overlooked where he stood. He wondered if Brian was there watching him now. He decided not to ring Brian's bell then. To visit him was the last thing on his mind now. He hastily moved off from the Mansions and hurriedly moved off down the street in the direction of Cold blow lane. He headed off towards the south to pay a visit to the Boswell's for now more than ever he needed to find Ruby.

Ruby Boswell paced the floors of the building looking for some way out. But all doors leading outside were securely locked. She opened doors where young women were involved in educational sessions led by men dressed in the same uniform as the Doctor. She opened other doors where women were receiving medical treatments on beds. They all looked as if they were drugged. Another room was extremely large surrounded by glass walls in which orchestral music was played and the furnishing were of plants and greenery. Here women were chanting words which she never heard in her life. On the walls of the corridors were the screens similar to the one shed seen in Terry's apartment. It all reminded her of the folk songs her father sang to her as a child. What were the words of that particular . Oh yes she remembered it now it was "Welcome to the hotel California once your booked in you can never leave".The anthem haunted her. Then she heard the loud man's voice out loud down the corridors. "This is a secure unit,we look after you all here and protect you from all the evils of the under ground". "You are safe here you are persons, you are individuals, you are unique and free". Just then she felt a hand on her shoulder, she looked around to see who it was. It was the Doctor he smiled that sick smile of his and then spoke to her. "I see you found your way then"? he said "Come into my office and rest Ruby, il send for a cup of pure tea for you caffeine free". He opened the office door and led her into the small room. She noticed there were no fittings or furniture. Apart from a tiny table and two hard chairs. "Please Sit down" he said. Then he pressed the button on the table and a short dark skinned woman appeared and he spoke to her "two teas Maria".

Mrs Dora Boswell was clearing the table she had eaten her lunch and put her husbands meal aside. He had not come home yet and she was beginning to get worried. Then she heard the door open and slam shut. "Where ave you been?" she said "ive had your dinner ready here for ages its not good enough". Mr Boswell entered the room and said "sorry my luv I was talking to my mates asking if they knew the whereabouts of our Ruby". "Seems she's disappeared" he said. "Its not like her to not tell us where she is". "I knew she was spending time with Terry I hope she's not been taken in by those city zone folk". Then Mrs Boswell spoke "so youv not heard anything from anyone?" she said. Then she said "ave you asked Bert if he knows where she is"?. Mr Boswell replied "Yes I did ask him but he hasn't seen her either since she signed in down the yard". Mrs Boswell said "Any ways you'd better eat your dinner afore it gets cold luv"Ben said "I will visit the show people later on the heath see if they know anything luv". He sat at the table and began eating the meal his wife had prepared for him. Just then there was a loud knock on the door. "Now whose that?" he asked. Mrs Boswell said, " il go and see, might be someone with news of our Ruby". She went to the door and opened it and was overjoyed to see that it was Terry. She greeted him warmly with a hug n kiss and said "Terry come in lad we was wondering if you'd seen our Ruby?". Terry walked into the room he looked worried. "I've not seen her for ages,was hoping she was here" he said. Ben spoke " No Terry we've not heard from her for days, thought perhaps she was with you". Terry replied"Well she was the other day, but she left me without telling me where she was going or why".

CHAPTER TWELVE

WAYS AND MEANS

WAYS AND MEANS

There are ways and means
beyond the scenes
of humanities dreams
there are tokens and absurdities
clothed in false securities

There are thousands upon thousands
too many to comprehend
they hide behind an illusion
waiting around the bend

Sometimes i see the master craft
sometimes i glimpsed their truth
sometimes i walk with angels
often i walk with clowns

You ask me
what's the difference my friend
youl just have to look around

There are ways and means to question
their answers are often so profound
yet he lost them in their visions
of justice, crime and vows

Ray Wills

ASSEMBLIES

They assembled at the Junction
'twixt heavens gate and hell
there were lots of soldier boys there
and Jonah at the well

The fallen undertaken
and the mystic dreamer who
proceeded to dictate a rhyme
like Mary and a shoe

Cinderella was in chains that night
and the doctor said a prayer
there were little children dancing
and i smelt the roses in her hair

The party poops were overboard
and the bibles were for free
when the showman called for peace that night
and graces victory

The tables turned to ashes
and the player sang his tune
the lofty words of Isaiah
and the shadows of the moon

The dogs they barked
and begged for food
and the crumbs fell to the floor
in the last road to forgiveness
and the knocker at the door

The words were spoke in Arabic
and the music hummed the reels
the meanings were just
a road to consequence
and the drinkers at the still

The birds of heaven flew there
and the prophets cried for peace
when the soldiers died of innocence
and the teacher tried to teach

The band it played the music
and all the people danced
but the words were lost in conflict there
like the sermons on the mount

Ray Wills

TIME FOR UNDERSTANDING

Its time for just a little understanding
no words no melody no soft refrains
no buck-board rides in the summer
no autumn tears in the wind and rain

No carousels to set you a dancing
no laughter voices to reclaim
just an old song left in my collection
to gather dust no tears or pain
Time for just a little understanding
long walks on the rivers edge
where songbirds offer their illusions
in melodies free of pain
The sunshine gal runs out to greet me
the children laugh and all is well
no shadows in my life of sorrows
just carousels and wishing wells

Tomorrows dreams are just like sun dust
where roses bloom around each door
i kissed her softly in the moonlight
how come she always asks for more.

Ray Wills

The doctor spoke, "Ruby you have a visitor" he said. The door of her dormitory swung open and an elderly man entered the room. He spoke "you may not remember me young lady, but you may have heard my name mentioned by your friend Terry Hewes". "My name is Brian Deleaux" he said. Ruby smiled then said,"oh yes your Terry's friend, he spoke a lot about you". "Have you heard from Terry?" she asked. "Can you let him know im here?" she asked. Brian walked across the room and took her hands in his and looked into her eyes. Then he spoke in a concerning way."There's things about Terry you should know" he said. "He's wanted by the good people of our community, seems he's on the run now!". "I'm afraid he's in serious trouble Ruby" he said." im trying to get in touch with him and help him, before its too late". Ruby asked,"Too late!, too late for what?" she asked. "How did you know I was here anyway?" she asked. Brian answered her "I am in a privileged position within the organisation" he said. "and I have access to most things" he said. He smiled at her and said "I can help you Ruby if your a good girl,your getting a lot better im told by the Doctor here and you may soon be able to return to the city zone". "We have a position ready for you, its your old position at the centre"he said. Then it dawned on her where she remembered him from. "Now I remember you" she said said "you were one of those at the centre who you used to watch all those shows of those naked women"she said. "You asked me for sexual favours too" she said. He stared at her then he smiled and said "yes, your right but you were there illegally at the time Ruby, before we found out and we had you removed. You were from a vagrant family"he said. Ruby spoke "Terry never knew that you were a top ranking official in the organisation there did he"?she asked. He answered her "No but he knew I was a member of high rank, just as he is a member and has a strong bearing on our aims and objectives". Then he said "Now that your back within our ranks we can help you throughout your life Ruby,you can be of great help to Terry too". Ruby listened to him but she didn't trust or like him. But she knew she would have to cooperate with him.

The high pitched siren sounded across the three pits in the yards of woodpecker. Workers from the brick yard,the pottery and the mine made their way to the gathering on the heath. The area had its tallest chimney in the locality and was where the goldfinches lived amongst the thorn bushes. During the autumn months there were regular fairgrounds here with stalls and shows. It was a regular meeting place a stopping place for travellers over the centuries. Here today there were many wagons, vardoa and the fine cobs grazing I the meadows nearby. Hundreds made their way here today. The air was full of noise and the sounds of people moving and talking. But above it all was the loud sound of the siren drowning any audible talk. Bert made his way to the top of the mound a position where he could speak to those hundreds gathered here. The procession of people made their way there up from the deepness. Bert knew what had to be said on this occasion an event which had never occurred before in his lifetime. His people the travellers had talked their folk "Says"around campfires for generations about the great strike of centuries past. Talked of the unions, men's rights,martyrs and the labouring people and the party. But such a thing was never discussed in depth before by this or previous generations of his people. Coming down to where he stood from another direction were many hundreds of members of the travelling show people. For the word had got around amongst them too. They tend our labour were here to support their brothers and sisters. After some considerable time and when most had gathered Bert Rogers spoke into the mic. "Good day brothers and sisters". A cheer went up from the vast crowd gathered there. Bert spoke,"I've brought you here for a purpose this is the very first time iv e had to call such a meeting and its for a very good reason". "As you know from our ancestral "Says" around the yog. we know about the great strikes of the past". "Those were generations ago when folks had life a lot harder than now". He continued,"However brick, pottery and coal remain essential to our way of life". "Today I'm calling this strike, that is to bring a halt to our present labour". He looked around at the audience the startled looks on their faces below. Then said."As you know the whole world relies on our industries as it always has done since the very first industrial revolution centuries ago". "Our forefathers taught us the importance of our labour, our skills in brick making, pottery and on the coal mines". "So that is why without further to do, today im giving you a treat". "I'm inviting a young man, one of rhesus a Hughes". "He's come here today to

121

speak to us today about our present situation, our masters and the dangers of the new World order." He turned and shook hands with Terry. Then he said,"This here's Terry Hughes please give him a warm welcome and listen to what he's got to say","Welcome Terry Hughes". Terry stood there looking down on the multitude of people. There were literally hundreds gathered here along with all their wagons and horses. Terry cleared his throat then he began his talk."Good morning ladies and gentlemen." "First a little about myself. "Although I have gypsy traveller ancestry as a young man I took the name Hewes spelt HEWES". "My father and mother were members of the city organisation known as the New World Order". "I was brought up to follow in my fathers footsteps and I was educated through the order". "When I was a young man I was a pioneer with an interest in mathematics and learning". "I had very actual little practical understanding of gypsy travellers". "Apart from that which I learned from the screens and those class of people which were known by the order as vagrants". "As far as I was concerned at that time I was taught that such people no longer existed in society".

"Then I like most were educated through the screen system whereby folk looked at moving pictures and words and heard talks".. "This way we were taught all the modern understandings that the old ways and lifestyles of past generations were all unhealthy, unsound, unsafe". "I myself took up and was established in a role of establishing an education programme" . "A Programme which showed the foolishness of such ways". "Our modern world enabled us to live a more positive constructive healthy life life expectancy increased greatly over the centuries". "We moved society away from that period known as childhood with all its foolish games, pastimes and play times". "The periods of infancy and after were greatly reduced and adult life took precedence", "Risk was to be completely eliminated and taken out of the equation". "With less stressful physical work environments replaced by robot lines and of course those who refused to take part". "We brought in corrective and correct thinking behaviour centres and had screens fitted in all homes and in communities to assist our people". "With healthier lives through correct diets no additives, spices, sauces, salt, sugars etc we were well in the process of creating a free new world order". Terry stopped talking before firmly stating "Now I want to bring you up to date". Just then there was a commotion within the crowds. Suddenly at the same time it seemed as of there was a circle of uniformed people and the sky above was full of menacing drones. All were making a buzzing noise which gave him a terrible penetrating headache and which made it difficult for him to think. He felt sick and giddy. It was then that Terry saw her moving in the crowd with the crowd of blue suited men behind her. She was moving eagerly towards him on the mound waving at him and excitedly calling out his name. "Terry Terry".It was his Ruby. Then all went black.

Terry Hewes woke from a long sleep with his head buzzing the bright artificial lights were shining directly down upon him,hurting his eyes. He wondered where he was and what day or time it was. He looked down to his wrist to his watch , but his watch with its phone was no longer there. In fact he was naked. He tried to remember what had happened and where he was. But he couldn't remember anything apart from the light in his eyes and the pain in his right arm. He looked at his arm, there was a mark there where the needle had gone in. He then remembered them holding him down, putting that hard thing into his mouth. He then renumbered the needle going into him and the apparatus being strapped upon his head. Then there was nothing. Apart from the dreams, dreams which were nightmares. Where voices told him that risks were everywhere he was to avoid them at all costs. He tasted something in his mouth his tongue burned and his head ached. Then he remembered her the girl who kissed him. He remembered her sweet lips upon his and him laying with him naked and her voice soft gentle and her movements upon him passionate and arousing. He remembered then her words of love and encouragement. She said "you must forget the way of life of my people and we will live together as a team Terry". "Because I love you"she said "The organisation is supreme my love, they will save us, trust me Terry". Yes it was her, it was Ruby and she loved him. He heard the man's voice again in his head and he felt the pain deep in his head again. Yet the doubts were still there along with the throbbing pain in his head.

It could have been hours or even days later that Brian entered the room. Terry heard his voice" good morning Terry," "Its your friend Brian,ive come to see if your feeling better". Terry looked at him in the light, he looked so different somehow. He was wearing one of those blue suits which the master wore with the familiar emblem of eagle and swallows in flight on the coat. Brian looked at Terry and asked him"How are you feeling now"? "would you like to talk Terry?". Terry looked at him and asked him "why are you here Brian?","and why am i here?", "what is this place?". Brian answered him, "Lots of questions Terry", "but il try to help you", "that's why im here!".Brian spoke "The Dr told me today Terry that they had to give you food through a straw at first, but your getting stronger now". "You had quite an ordeal!", "that crowd charging you like that!". "They are still not behaving"he said "Unfortunately we had to liquidise many". Terry was shocked by what he said. "What do you mean you had to liquidate them?" he asked. Brian replied. "Well, its like I said Terry the organisation had no alternatives in the end and felt it would make it a safer place if such vagrants anti social devils were not around to influence the decent responsible members of society". He continued his explanation "Of course we needed the workforce in their skills to create the great foundations for our structural networks of our zones.".." He continued to speak"they were more than happy to live in such conditions and we up till now have kept such things from our people in the new world order". "Bricks,pottery and heat were essential fabric to all things,they always have been". He carried on his talk "These people and the Gypsy vagrants were able to come and go in their own world quite happy for centuries, without spoiling our own growth and development". "We have with you and others, managed to developed ideas and support and been able to advance our society greatly". He then smiled at Terry and asked Terry. "Did you enjoy your time with your girl?".Terry looked at him with disgust and distrust all in one expression. "You mean Ruby don't you?" he said. Brian smiled again then said "Yes Terry, I mean Ruby", "you never told me about your little sex nest with her did you Terry?" he asked. Terry replied " No, I thought you found out through your false mechanical goldfinches which you created didn't you"? he asked. Brian smiled and replied "Yes your right Terry, they've been one of my major successes for the organisation". "As far as Ruby is concerned, yes that's her name", "she's a good girl and assures us that you will co operate with us, as you love her", "she's also had her special training now for a few weeks and no longer has bad thoughts" "and is preparing a suite in our centre for you and her to live there together". "She's got her old job back too" "We want you both to be very happy"."We want you onboard again and were offering you great things". "We have taken on board your last report Terry and are progressing well in implementing your suggestions". "Though we still have to resolve the strike in the underground which Bert Rogers instigated". "We are hopeful you can help us there Terry we are expecting great things of you!". "I will leave you now Terry lad youv a lot to think over, no doubt our Dr here will be able to help you through all this". "When your ready Terry come and see me at the Mansions and we can discuss things in more detail".Then he left the room.

After Brian had left Terry tried to get his head together. He still had the headaches and the reoccurring thought that the organisation was trouble. He was coming to the realisation that Brian was actually the head of the organisation. Along with the realisation that the man he'd seen weeks earlier was just a deputy there a decoy to keep him off the track.

In the Boswell household all was not well. Mrs Boswell was busy trying to make what little food she had feed her and her husband. Mrs Boswell spoke "Cant understand it Ben have heard no hide or hair from our Ruby? ".Ben answered her "I tried to tell you women she's a turncoat, she got back to work in that snotty town club place". His wife spoke again, "I never did like her working there Ben,why couldn't she stay with us n help Bert down at the Yards"?. Ben answered her annoyingly,"What's up with you woman?" "I told you woman, since we been out on the strike there's no work for anyone." "cause that's the idea of striking to make them pay for what they done". "They need all our bricks, pots, tiles and coal cause without it all their buggered"!. Mrs Boswell turned on him and answered him herself getting rather angry too,"Don't you use that language here Ben Bosvill"(she always used that term when she was cross with him).She spoke again "I wont have it, we may be poor, but we be respectable folk". Ben Boswell spoke, "I

Know you do come from them Stanley's down south woman, but their no more posh than we are". "Any ways them their people took that young Terry fella the other week at our meeting they dragged him away, it was all fault of our Ruby she led them to him". He sounded very upset. "There was nowt we could do at the time they had those machines in the sky and we were surrounded", "Lot our folk just disappeared in thin air after they people sprayed some toxic stuff around us". "Twas Lucky Bert didn't get it too" he said.

It was midday when Terry was released from the medical recovery unit. He had spent some 6 weeks all told there. The treatment and training he received there they considered was more than adequate. All of the medical health team considered him cured of his sickness and fully recovered from his ordeal at the Yard. During that time there he had had regular visits from Ruby who had assisted in his programme of recuperation and re education. He was as stated in the doctor Johnston's report of sound mind and health and ready to face the challenges of the world face on. Ruby arrived early that day and met him in the hall of the medical and education centre. After he'd said farewell to the Doctor and staff. He was fitted out with the regular uniform of the organisation with its eagle and birds emblem and together Ruby and him stepped outside into the bright late summer sunlight. Just as they did so,there was that familiar sound of horses hooves and cartwheels turning. Then a familiar voice called out to Terry "Cmon Mush quick jump on board". It was Bert Rogers. Once they were both onboard the vardo wagon they headed up out of the zone and headed towards the south east of the city. Bert turned to Terry and said with a chuckle "They are all ready and they are all expecting you, even your Mum and Dad Ruby". Terry held Ruby close to him and smiled. He looked at Bert then asked him,"Will we be playing any games Bert ?" he asked. Bert answered with a big grin "Sure lots, as all the kids of all ages are coming along all with their bats, balls, ropes and hoops". "Even little four balls Mary Donnelly from down the avenue was asking after you, and the young man who runs the junk playground will be there".

CHAPTER THIRTEEN

EXPLOSIVE

STRANGER DAYS

There were people gathered there
from all walks of life
a guy on a horse
and a boy on a bike

A girl selling daisies
in strings to delight
and a lady in disguise
with a bosom to please
for the young men's delights

The ringmaster showman
he wore a tall hat
the Yankee ballplayer
sported a bat

The music played loud
from an old fashioned band
the conductor was drunk
with bent baton in hand

The clown and the jester
both came out to play
along with the rogues
from the fools hideaways

The sunshine was bright
but the thunder was loud
as the little girl cried

and the drunk wet his pants
Whilst the Gypsies
had once all travelled
from New York to France

It was a day to remember
and a time to recall
when the maids trimmed their wicks
and the Lord had a ball

The castanets clicked
and the violins played
when the teetotallers drank
and the farmers made hay
in the great big parade

The lights in the shadows
danced to delight
whilst the frog and the toad
got into a fight

Then the phantoms came out
in the broad light of day
whilst the opera played on
and the brave ran away

The topics and antics
were preached to the poor
while the widows and wise men
all shut their doors

Ray Wills

THOUGHTS OF THE TOMORROWS

Censored like robots
gathered in chains
in the streets of the cities
alleys and lanes

Masked and forsaken
within all of their dreams
ordered and cautioned
mandatory scenes

Prophets and poets
writers of pen
scholars and dreamers
was science to blame

Zealots and criminals
ranked all in line
distances measured
brothers and sisters divine

Clusters and crazies
lock down in halls
children in masks
all
followed the law

Like corrupted soldiers
they all stood in line
boozers and rebels
some full of hope
others took whispers
shrouded in dope

In thoughts of tomorrows
give them the rope

Ray Wills

Terry Hewes was sat in his studio deep in thought. How wonderful it had all worked out with Ruby's people and all those at the yards had returned to work. The strike after all was a success and the work conditions and the output had both increased for the better. His role with the organisation had taken on more responsibility and the organisations future was sound. Ruby was with him living in the suite working at the centre and all was well. Or was it?. Something was troubling him and had been for a while. Those strange thoughts were returning, his mind was getting confused about things again. Thoughts about taking risks and questioning his own judgement bothered him. Some nights recently he had had recurring dreams about pastimes and play. He thought back to the day he and Ruby had come to the welcoming return party with Bert at the yard. That day when he himself had been to put in the position to enable to offer all those at the brick works,the pottery and the mine such good futures, under the organisation. Brian had suggested to him that he Terry was now in a privileged position to win them all over and he had. Hadn't he?.After all it was all for the best wasn't it?.After all the workforce had won and the organisation had too. Still there was something not quite right. Something was really troubling him.

He kept having recurring images in his head of hordes of children playing in a playground. All playing dangerously with tools. Whilst others were climbing up ropes and hurtling down steep wooden chutes to the hard earth below. There were children playing dangerously around blazing fires, others eating charcoaled burnt potatoes. Others kicking a ball around, pushing and tripping one another over. Children were darting backwards and forwards with some tripping over and bruising their knees. And all of them in need of a good body scrubbing. But what was peculiar was they all had permanent smiles on their faces. Whilst many were laughing and all of them seemed to be very happy and contented. He couldn't understand why they were all involved in risky pursuits pastimes covered in dirt and yet they were in a state of bliss. It was as if they were drugged in euphoria. These were boys and girls of all ages from small tots just walking to lanky teenagers were involved possible hundreds, in a less than one acre site. There were no adults or to be seen here just one tall youth the elder. Who though gave the impression of being in charge yet he never controlled nothing or stopped their activities. No mater their danger and yet no one seemed to get seriously hurt that was the amazing thing. He then remembered,it all came back to him, for this was the scene he had witnessed once in the avenue by the subways yet it seemed a lifetime ago now. But as he remembered all of this, his head ached and he remembered the bright light in his eyes. He remembered too, the taste in his mouth, the jabs in his arm and the apparatus they had clamped onto his head then the horrific pains. He dozed to sleep then when he awoke some hours later the pains were gone. It was late afternoon and Ruby was by his side on the bed. "Your were dreaming" she said "you were talking in your sleep too". He smiled at her and reached out for her. But she was distant and looked annoyed. "What's up" he asked "nothing,nothings wrong" she replied. But he knew her too well to know that she was lying. He asked again "What's wrong".She frowned then replied "its you Terry, you seemed to be so distant lately and you said stuff in your dreams" she said. "I cant help my dreams" he replied. She said "its not just that Terry ", "Brian's concerned that you may be getting ill again"she said. He was annoyed now and asked her. "Have you discussed me with him?"he asked. She replied "Of course, I always do, because I love you and worry about you, especially when your not thinking right". "So im not thinking right" he said. Ruby moved from the bed then she said " Look Terry ive got to go to the centre now wel talk later" and then she was gone. He lay there for a while. Why has it all gone so wrong he wondered. He got up from the bed and made his way across the room. It was a brilliant suite more room then his previous apartment and with a bigger window with splendid view across Greenwich park. He walked over to his screen and pressed the button. It was a larger screen much larger than his old one and was quicker. He pressed a few buttons then he typed in the words "RUBY CORDELL" and then the picture came up with her profile. The profile included her work record for the organisation. Along with her personal details,he saw that she had him down there as her partner. He typed in a few more words and the machine came up with the word and also said the word "PROHIBITED". This really threw him. It was so unexpected. Strange he thought that he'd once again been denied access to her

131

security. As he knew that she was cleared, retrained and accepted as an official member of the organisation. He began to consider that her info was just prohibited from him alone. Which meant they were monitoring his own access. Which was worrying. He wondered how much she had picked up from listening in on his dreams. Surely she didn't know what he was thinking. He trusted her, but now he knew he had to be extra careful, for even Ruby could turn his world upside down. He knew that his present thinking, did not comply with even his own earlier work and reports. Now he knew had discovered that the world outside of the new world order had some rational thinking behaviour which he now realised was truly unique and so special. He thought of the meals he had eaten at the Boswell's and how they were so enjoyable compared to the tasteless morsels from the kitchen compote . He remembered the warmth he had felt in their living room. The feeling he felt from the coal fire and the sight of just looking its its red embers coal, He remembered the taste of the sweet tea and how it made him feel. So unlike the watery tea which he drank from the glass bottles. He remembered how aged her parents were. Yet there was a distinctness of age which made him feel comfortable. He rememberer how all the children in the avenue were of many ages. From infants to young youths every age group in fact yet within had their own identity and ways of movement, physical appearance and distinct speech. These he realised were all unique. These great important attributes were all lacking in the new world order. Whilst in the work yards he recalled that the men, women and children all worked together as a unity, as a family. This was not permitted in the modern world. He realised now that he had been involved in the making and operation of a monstrous system. A system which controlled, limited and devalued mankind. He felt sick and ashamed that he had contributed to its development. It had taken his journey into the prohibited area the under world of the yards and avenues to discover the reality of it all. To discover the real truth.

Brian Deleaux clocked into his screen like he did most mornings. He said "Good morning Robert." But this time something wasn't quite right. His screen lit up and showed the word and the voice said "PROHIBITED". It was like a bad dream!. Nothing like this had occurred before in all the years he had been with the organisation. He pressed the overdrive and the words came up along with the voice speech, "Your machine has been hacked". "Please check your main line". He hurriedly pressed his password in and the information came up. It showed all the information on the organisation, its aims and objectives. but this time it was all so different. Someone had over rolled the system. Not just his personal info, but the whole of the organisations aims and objectives, its rules and procedures. It had all been changed it was now all rewritten. He did not recognise any of it. Someone or some other body had tapped into it. They had gained access to all documentation and removed the mother board programme and replaced it with a new one. One that was entirely contrary to the organisation in which he had known and controlled and one that he had operated as its head for decades. This was dangerous. This was a bad dream. This was a nightmare. Brian was shaking as he slipped his micro phone out of his wristwatch and dialled the number. A woman's voice answered, "Yes Brian what is it?"she asked. "Its happened, someone's done it" he said.

Terry Hewes was tired. He had been up all night working on the system. Ruby had come back earlier in the night and had crashed out on the spare bed. He was glad she was sleeping as he didn't want to confront her and needed time to complete the task. He had made copies of everything and had studied the importance of brick works,pottery and fuel in the original industrial revolution of centuries past. He knew how the whole structural foundations of society was based upon this understanding. He knew that the Gypsy workforce, his ancestors and others had all these particular skills. He had studied the stone masonry and the Freemasons Guilds, craftsmen that they were. He knew most of the organisations philosophy and objectiveness. As he himself had been involved in its growth in recent years with his reports and recommendation, most of which were implemented. He had now known of these and of the value and importance of play. The pastimes of people and the importance of that relationship with energy and the importance of risk in all of life's activities. He also now was well aware of the need for pleasure from food. These were he had come to realise were the greatest of joys. Along with all its tastes and enjoyment. Its values at shared mealtimes with others and not just eating alone. Along with the pleasure from sharing moments in time of sitting around a fire. Also he now knew of the joys of water such as splashing in puddles and water play. All of these he had studied in a short period of time as his mind was set free. He had set to work all that night and into the early hours and by the early hours it was completed. He had changed it all for the better. Most of the old methods doctrines and laws were eradicated such as the lethal injections and liquidisation. Travelling people were now free to roam and children to play. Weather control and gender bending was unlawful Male and Female genders were once again of separate value and had equal rights. Some of the modern life styles remained such as clean air and fuel, The work was finished but could be added to improved by others. And now he lay on his bed and slept.

Ruby's phone rang and she answered it. It was Brian. "Yes Brian, what is it?" she asked. "Why are you phoning me now Brian?.I've only just woke" she said. Brian answered her, "its happened someone's done it" he said "I'm phoning you because your the only one I can trust Ruby and the only one who could possibly do this is him". "Who Brian? what's happened? she asked "Its Terry of course." he said. "Why what's happened? "What's he done " she asked. Brian replied, "Someone's got into our system and altered everything" "I cant access none of the original info" he said. "It must be him, as he knows his way around these things" "A lot of it on there, especially the most recent documentation was created by him" he said. "Are You sure its him? "she asked him "well not really," he said. She spoke, "Well he's fast asleep on the bed here now Brian". "I just saw him, he's well out of it, surely it cant be him, I cant see its him Brian" she said. He answered her. "Well, can you see what you can find out from him Ruby?", "You know ive been concerned about him", "especially after you told me recently his behaviour isn't right". She answered him, "OK Brian il get back to you later". "Hope your able to resolve this Brian, there must be someone else in the team who can help to resolve this". Brian sighed and said, "Yes I hope so too", "otherwise the whole network and organisation will be in serious trouble!" . "This is Explosive." he said Then he rang off and slid his micro phone back into his wrist watch. He was very worried and he was shaking uncontrollably.

Terry Hewes woke up from his long sleep. It was midday and it was raining heavy outside. He could hear it beating down on the windows of his apartment. He lay there gathering his thoughts. Then he remembered. He remembered just all that he had done and smiled to himself. He heard Ruby moving around in the next room. She was busy on the screen. He wondered how they would react. No doubt Brian would panic. But how would Ruby take it, no doubt she was now on the screen and reading all the new information he'd created. All of the new doctrine of the organisation. He wondered if she would really know what he had done. The significance of it all. Would she realise it was his work alone or believe it was work of other members in the team. Would she follow the code of practice set out on the screen,like everyone else no doubt would. He had worked tirelessly in creating the philosophy, its ideals and way of life set out for all members of the organisation. He had no doubts that all the members of the organisation would carry on following the screens directions as they had always done. They were all conditioned to follow the guidelines. As they always had done for they never ever questioned the New World Order.

CHAPTER FOURTEEN

GRAND FINALE

A DAY TO REMEMBER

It was a day to remember and never forget
when our music was playing and she wore that Rosette
the sun it was shining and the lambs were at play
the children were singing in the warm summers day

It was a day like no others when the church bells did chime
when the rabbits did scramble from their warrens divine
when the birds sang their melodies and the lizards did squirm
when the squirrel searched for nuts by the old barn n worn

There were apples in the orchards and blossoms on boughs
the leaves were so green and the maids milked the cows
the streams and the rivers were all flowing free
where the hayricks were high with a view to the sea

The people were dancing and the band struck the chords
there were Gypsies and hippies praising the lord
the hills told their story like the artist at play
when God shared his glory in the great light of day

Ray Wills

FOLLOW THAT DREAM

I'm going to follow my dreams
across the new highways
where the rivers flow free
and there's peace and liberty
I'm going to walk on the tracks
where poets once roamed
I'm going to count all my blessings
and im going to roam
then im heading home

I'm going to search for the treasures
I'm going to speak to the dames
I'm going preach to the sinners
that love is the game

I'm going to light a new candle
and say a new prayer
I'm going to sail from my harbour
to be with her there

I'm going to follow my heart
to where it belongs
I'm going to be faithful
and im gonna be strong

I'm going to follow the pathways
where poets have trod
I'm going to bask in the sunshine
walk on the sod

I'm going to build a new frontier
where the Indians once roamed
im going to fashion my poetry
cause im heading home

I'm going to follow my dreams
lift anchor and sail
I'm counting the days now
im begging at the well
I'm counting my blessings
from daybreak to dusk
I'm singing that song now
to those i can trust

I'm following that dream
along the new trail
they've been there before me
I can sense their grand spell

I'm following those trail blazers
those old timers writ
I'm rocking and rolling
sure got me some hit

I'm following my dreams
im counting the days
I'm praising my lord there
and im whispering the page
I'm following those dreams
afore im waylaid

Ray Wills

WHERE FREEDOM REIGNS

Pathfinders and seekers
through old country lanes
turnings and heathlands
through many life's games

Campfires and vardos
all there to delight
like the dew in the mornings
and starlight at night

Forever journeys
and rich tales to share
rivers and valleys
promises and prayers

There was dancing of children
barefoot and free
songs of the heathers
amidst birch and wide leas

All Roma nomadic
travellers free
like the sparks of the fire
through all eternity

The Gypsy Queen smiles
amidst the horses neat reins
celebrate freedoms of mankind
in sunshine and rains

Furze bush and bracken
in country to roam
forever nomadic
for freedoms their home

Ray Wills

WORLD GONE WRONG

Where the flag flies and the liberty statue speaks
where freedom reigns in the double speech
across the pacific ocean and the rivers of antiquity
where truth was born and men are free

The native clad in his true worth
amongst noble men of royal birth
where the eagle flies and the stars are rich
on the banner reads where the wise men sit

On the plains of glory and the battlegrounds
the bugle boy sounds the last retreat
in the land of honey and McDonald meat
the orators of men in foolish gain
reflect and share their wise refrains

Across the world of greed and power
the seas of glory and the Eiffel tower
the cross of Jesus and the walks of saints
the words of poets and the songs of John
crafted in vision and a world gone wrong

Ray Wills

SYSTEMS TEMPLERS TABERNACLE AND FOOLS

He was put there by popular choice
a man of the people
the theme and the voice
His was the reason they all walked in line
the wise and the free the rhymes and the Vines
The congressmen idioms
the men of the plains
the old schoolboy rhetoric
and the forgotten names

His was the vision
and the last bugle call
when the hands that were raised
were lost in the fall

The masters of doctrines
and the worldly and wise
the schools where they taught
where the seals were surmised

The handshakes and false flags
and the sayings they spout
the rivers of lies
and the truth it is out

Oh the masters of wars
and the doctrine of peace
in the temples of grace
where the crooked tongues preached

Where the bible was held
in high revelry
but they said
it was all just a ruse
to control you and me.

Ray Wills

THE LONG ROAD WELL TRAVELLED

Its a long road iv travelled
its a long beaten track
where the hills are a calling
for there's no going back
Its a long prayer ive whispered
its a long ways to go
over sweet rolling meadows
and well beating tracks
its a long ways from home

Where love knows no reason
and where the true Gypsy roams
its a long road a travelled
its a story im told
from the mouths of blind children
from the pens of lost souls

Its a long ways to travel
afore we meet again
so il tell you your fortune
afore i took you on home

Its a long write im writing
a heavy pen to dip
where the ink it lays weary
and the nib ends too quick

Its a long road ive travelled
through cities and bends
around cottages thatching
and old men called Ben

Its a long ways a travelling
through thickets and moss
where the harvests are a plenty
from the coins that ive tossed

Ray Wills

Terry Hughes had never imagined just how things would be so very different in his wildest dreams. He had hoped. But at the time he had actually put his plan into operation there was no way that he would envisage the full extent and benefits of the changes which he had made. His work had really come into fruition. Far greater for the good than he had ever anticipated. He knew that there were so many things needed changing. To think it all had evolved from his tripping over Ben Boswell that day. Then meeting Ruby and discovering the under world of the yards and all the children on the avenue through Mary Donnelly and their playtimes. Then what really changed him was his discovery of the goldfinch birds at Brian's apartment at the Mansion. For it was then when he really understood and it all began to take shape in his head. He soon begun to piece it all together, but he knew that he needed to work fast. His knowledge and his own involvement of the way that the organisation operated was proved to be most useful and profound. Then once he replaced the systems network with his own. Based upon the reality of the world outside of the New World Order he knew it would work. But he never realised just how all of the systems people would readily accept it all. And accept it all they did overnight. He thought back to that day three months ago now. When he woke up and realised just what he'd done and then all that happened on that day and the days that followed ever since. It was incredible, unbelievable and thank goodness that the alternative way which he had implemented proved to be so very successful. There were so very many benefits now. He reflected back to that very first day and he remembered.

Terry Hughes felt her body next to him on the bed, he felt her arms around him and her lips softly kissing his neck. "Your wonderful" she said "I love you Terry". "Thank you for everything" she said. Then she told him about Brian and the latest news. She said "I've just logged into the screen and Brian's gone, he's no more". Terry turned over on the bed facing her and looked into her eyes and said "What do you mean he's gone?" he asked. Ruby replied! "He took his life this morning Terry, he phoned me first then couldn't handle the shame of losing the power".

Then she said cheerfully, "Everyone's coming onto the streets they are all celebrating, its a new day".

He remembered that day how his phone had rang constantly with many congratulating him throughout the day. Ruby joined him on the streets outside. People who had been prisoners in their apartments came out onto the streets for the first time. Folks hugged one another and danced to the music played by many Gypsy bands. Mary 4 balls Donnelly ran to greet him and during the day taught him how to juggle and sing the all the words of the street rhymes. All of the children came up from the avenues and subways. Ruby was reunited with her mum and dad Mr and Mrs Boswell. People lit street fires celebrated and played games all day with the children. Libraries were open and books were read all of those previously banned.

Later in the evening Terry and Ruby talked. Terry explained about the new screen layout. It being all inclusive with the importance of risk built into the system. But most important was the fact that everyone now had freedom of choice in all areas of their life. Ruby had also told him the history of the Rose Tattoo and its origins and throughout the weeks and months that followed people had embraced the New World Order.

RECOMMENDED READINGS

ADVENTURES IN CHILDS PLAY - RAY WILLS - AMAZON

TIMES GONE - BY ROBERT DAWSON

ADVENTURE PLAYGROUNDS - JACK LAMBERT -
PENGUINS

CHILDRENS RHYMES IN STREETS AND PLAYGROUND

BY IONA AND PETER OPIE

HOW CHILDREN LEARN
BY JOHN HOLT

HOW CHILDREN FAIL
By JOHN HOLT

BRAVE NEW WORLD
BY ALDOUS HUXLEY

NINETEEN EIGHTY FOUR
BY GEORGE ORWELL

WHERE THE RIVER BENDS
BY RAYMOND WILLS

SUMMERHILL
BY A S NEIL

THE COMPLETE WORKS OF CHARLES DICKENS

SOMETHING EXTRAORDINARY
BY H S TURNER

Printed in Great Britain
by Amazon

78060465R00093